THE GOLEM OF BROOKLYN

THE
GOLEM
OF
BROOKLYN

| A NOVEL |

ADAM MANSBACH

ONE WORLD
NEW YORK

A One World Trade Paperback Original

Copyright © 2023 by Giants of Science, Inc.

Published in the United States by One World, an imprint of Random House, a division of Penguin Random House LLC, New York.

ONE WORLD and colophon are registered trademarks of Penguin Random House LLC.

LIBRARY OF CONGRESS CATALOGING-IN-PUBLICATION DATA
Names: Mansbach, Adam, author.
Title: The golem of Brooklyn : a novel / by Adam Mansbach.
Description: First edition. | New York : One World, [2023]
Identifiers: LCCN 2023018848 (print) |
LCCN 2023018849 (ebook) | ISBN 9780593729823 (paperback) |
ISBN 9780593729830 (Ebook)
Subjects: LCSH: Golem—Fiction. | Jews—New York
(State)—New York—Fiction. | Jewish mythology—Fiction. |
LCGFT: Humorous fiction. | Satirical literature. | Novels.
Classification: LCC PS3613.A57 G65 2023 (print) |
LCC PS3613.A57 (ebook) | DDC 813/.6—dc23/eng/20230519
LC record available at https://lccn.loc.gov/2023018848
LC ebook record available at https://lccn.loc.gov/2023018849

Printed in Canada on acid-free paper

oneworldlit.com

2 4 6 8 9 7 5 3 1

First Edition

Book design by Susan Turner

For Jamie

THE GOLEM OF BROOKLYN

Four Hundred Pounds of Clay

Len Bronstein was not so much in need of a golem as he was in possession of a large quantity of clay, and very stoned. Three hours earlier, after his morning coffee and in lieu of breakfast, he had eaten a hazelnut lace cookie containing twenty milligrams of THC, the last of a batch his friend Waleed had baked and brought to Len's Memorial Day cookout a few weeks earlier. Waleed did this regularly—it was how he expressed love, and also how he gained new customers. The nature of an event was always fundamentally altered by Waleed's arrival. It was awesome.

For the last several years, Len had been stealing one five-pound brick of premium sculpting clay each week from the private high school in Brooklyn Heights where he worked as an art teacher. He didn't really know why. Len liked his job, liked his co-workers, got along fine with his students—both the merely wealthy and famous actors' kids. Had Len asked, his department head probably would have invited him to take home all the clay he wanted. The school was awash in resources of every sort: the filmmaking lab had professional-grade cameras and editing suites, the fifth grade math teachers had PhDs. If Len had been fortunate enough to attend a school like this, he never would have ended up a high school art teacher.

Len was no sculptor; his artistic disciplines were not-painting and not-writing, which made the vast reserve of clay stacked up in the shed in the backyard all the more perplexing. But as Waleed's cookie—and with it, Waleed's genius—hit him full force, Len walked out of his garden apartment and into his apartment's garden, and the splintering, hard-to-latch door of the shed listed open, affording him a glimpse of the wall of light gray clay, and Len decided that today was the day to begin writing the masterwork of speculative fiction he'd been sketching out in his head, here and there, for the last however-many months.

The concept of the novel was that in the very near future, the study of epigenetics—the notion that trauma can be passed down in the DNA, can ramify across generations—takes a massive leap forward when an NYU biologist named Henry Kazinsky happens upon the work of a UC Berkeley anthropologist named Desiree Parrish, and they get to talking, and six years later they're married and six years after that they publish a paper in a peer-reviewed journal announcing that they can isolate and time-stamp extreme epigenetic traumas, pinpoint the historical moment they enter the DNA. He is the grandson of Polish Jews who watched everyone they knew incinerated at Treblinka; her people are descended from Ashanti warriors kidnapped and forced into slavery in Jamaica who escaped into the hills, intermarried with the indigenous Arawak population, and waged war against the Spanish and then the British and became known as Maroons, from a Spanish word that means "cannot be tamed." The media runs with these family histories, the very personal nature of the work.

The book they write is an instant bestseller. They almost hadn't published it at all, they reveal on a morning talk show. They know all the ways biology has fueled racism in the past, and they understand that their findings will be thrown into the great centrifuge of the culture, spun and tumbled into bludgeons. But it's not theirs to withhold the progress they have made—not out of fear.

Also, they're about to become billionaires.

Sure enough, two opposing arguments soon march forth from their respective strongholds to meet and do battle on the opinion pages, the political shows, the last bastardized bastions of discourse. Both take for granted that epigenetic testing will soon be as ubiquitous as DNA testing—remarkable in its own right, since nobody had ever heard of it a week before.

The conservative position is that epigenetic trauma is a disability—a disqualifier. Now that we know how real the damage is, we are morally obligated to take it seriously, and that means having a real conversation about how much responsibility someone quantifiably *damaged* ought to be given. *And no one is talking about sterilization here, Matt, but you have to really think, do we want to pass these kinds of things on to our children? We can't fix the past, but we can fix the future. And at the very least, that starts with transpar-*

ency. With knowing who among us may have experienced so much ancestral . . . oh jeez, what's the right word . . . so much difficulty *that they might be at an elevated risk for, and the science isn't in on this yet, but an elevated risk of mental illness, or heart disease, or, I don't know, a predisposition to violence. I mean, wouldn't you want to know if a person with those—are we calling them markers?—with those markers was teaching your kids, or representing you as an elected official? Or, gosh, even sitting across the table from you on a first date?*

The opposing argument is about *amends. Reparations* tests poorly with focus groups—too loaded, too closely associated with an argument that had never gathered steam—but *amends* is not so fraught. Surely, now that we're no longer speaking in abstractions, no longer speculating about whether the past lives inside us, now that we can finally agree on that much, we can turn to more fruitful discussions. We should be talking about a systematic way of compensating those whose ancestors have passed along the cellular records—the receipts—of their debasement. *The governments and corporations who have been on the brutalizing side of history would do well to get out in front of this, Mark. I can envision, for example, a situation where the U.S. says Okay, from 1619 to 1865, we had chattel slavery, so if you're an American of African descent and your epigenetic marker appears during those years, you're entitled to something. Or if you're a European Jew and your epigenetic marker appears between 1933 and 1945, then the German government—*

But hold on, Michelle—if you're a European Jew, what if you've already got an epigenetic marker from 1492, when your family was kicked out of Spain, or 1306, when they were kicked out of France, or 1096, when the Crusades started, or—

Well, that's why we need a system, Mark. So the courts aren't overwhelmed. Maybe we say, okay, you have a five-year window of time to get tested, and after that the books are closed. Maybe your settlement indemnifies the government or the corporation against any claims by your descendants. And I would think that just for the financial stability of the world, these would not be lump sum payments, but spread out over some number of years . . .

A month later, the first epigenetics case reaches the Supreme Court, and the justices rule 5–4 to enshrine plaintiffs' right to sue for ancestral trauma. Epigenetic testing centers spring up all over the country; transnational regulations are erected to preserve the interests of the too-big-to-fail.

Then somebody figures out how to transplant epigenetic markers from a donor to a recipient—a seller to a buyer. The DNA of each person who goes for testing is on file, so double-dipping is not an option. Choosing to sell means forgoing your claim.

Buyers pay twenty cents on the dollar, but they pay up front. Some cash in their claims immediately; others are hedging, stashing, waiting to see how the pendulum will swing. Sellers are more cynical; they presume that the trauma-makes-you-less-than position will win out. Better to sell high and stay off the radar, the registry.

Then buyers start to experience the genetic memories of the donors. The implantation process activates these dormant ancestral horrors, decades or centuries old, each one the discrete experience of a single person: the night the village burned, the day a child was caged or a parent sold away. These memories begin to drive people insane—to commit suicide in some cases, especially in the early months before the phenomenon is understood.

The revelation that recipients can access these memories directly births a secondary black market, with buyers selling the sellers' histories back to them—if they can find each other, because all this is highly illegal and everybody's identity is shielded. Other buyers begin to feel a growing conviction that what is in their bodies is theirs now—to own, to claim, to talk about. Have they not now, in some way, become survivors of slavery, exile, experimentation, holocaust?

A surrogacy market springs up next, allowing people who would rather know the origins of their trauma than receive amends for it pay to implant it into others—who then assume the burden and perform the telling. From these transactions is born a religious sect, the Trauma Eaters. They believe in consuming as much trauma as possible as a form of penance, though they prove useless in relaying the information back to the sellers, because all the competing trauma fries their brains.

Len intended to explore this world by telling the story of an epic journey by a woman who gets tested, fully expecting to find epigenetic trauma markers, and instead finds none. This so thoroughly obliterates her understanding of herself that weeks later she becomes a buyer, hoping in some desperate, half-understood way that this will restore her self-identity. When the memories begin to manifest, she sees something not just horrible, but personal, and actionable—something that will change the world, if only she can track down the person from whose DNA these memories were extracted.

But Len could never figure out what that thing could be. This was why he had not written a word.

This was *one* reason he had not written a word.

And upon further reflection, this was not the day to start.

He walked across the yard, threw open the shed door, and stared at all that clay.

Golemology

Of all the supernatural creatures in Jewish folklore, the golem is basically the only decent one: a giant humanoid built of mud or clay, always by a learned and holy man, and always in a time of crisis. The Hebrew word for truth is inscribed on its forehead, certain esoteric prayers and rituals are incanted and enacted, and the golem animates. Talmudic scholars, who agree on nothing, are unanimous in rejecting the notion that the golem is *alive*.

When the golem has accomplished its mission—typically the martial defense of the Jewish people (as was the case with the Golem of Prague, widely considered the Michael Jordan of golems), but sometimes manual labor (the task appointed to the Golem of Chelm, usually regarded as the Scottie Pippen of golems)—the aleph is erased from his forehead, changing the word *truth* to the word *death* and causing the golem to return to a state of vacant immobility, like a toddler in front of a television screen.

Why there has not been a greater profusion of golems, given the number of extremely shitty situations in which the Jewish people have found themselves over the last fifty-seven hundred and eighty-three years, remains a mystery. But clues might be found in the literature of golems, which you can read about on the internet.

In some tellings, the golem is a heroic savior. In others, he is an uncontrollable monster, a doltish brute, even a tragic lover. But perhaps we have not yet scratched the surface of what the golem means.

Avu Iz Mayn Shmok

Len scratched the surface of his golem, bending over the supine form with a wooden chopstick in his hand and etching the Hebrew letters into the golem's heavy, clumsily made brow. He checked his work frequently against the translation website open on his laptop, balanced atop the golem on the cement part of the backyard. Hebrew was not a language Len knew; he had grown up observant only in the sense that he noticed things.

The golem's body was chunked with slabs of muscle up and down its four-hundred-pound, nine-and-a-half-foot length. Len was immensely proud of the golem's shoulders, which were filigreed with remarkably realistic-looking striations along the deltoids. The hands were artless, and the feet looked like a pair of cinderblocks the golem had decided to wear as bedroom slippers. The face was brutal and amateurish, but expressive—the broad lips eager to peel back in a snarl or a laugh, the deep-set eyes oddly cagey and alert. The ears looked like actual clumps of sun-bleached dog shit that someone had decided to glue to a human head, but they were Len's eighth attempt at ears and enough was enough.

It was dark now, and Len's only break had been four hours ago, to wolf down a takeout container of pad see ew while scouring the internet for phonetic English renderings of the incantations and secret names of God he needed to recite to fill the golem's lungs—Len had not made lungs—with the breath of life. Naturally, there was no consensus to be found on which prayers were the proper ones or which secret names were real. Len thought highly of his ability to discern good information from bad, but whether those skills translated to the arena of online Jewish mysticism was yet to be determined. He had taken his best shot: spoken what might be the right words, walked the prescribed number of circles around his creation, mixed his own blood with dirt from a cemetery and dipped his chopstick in the gunk and used it to scrawl the all-important letters, the last of which he was completing now.

Technically, the dirt wasn't from a cemetery, just a corner of the yard. But what was a cemetery? Just a place where something dead was buried, and a bee or worm or dinosaur had almost certainly died here at some point in history and decomposed into this soil. This logic, like the golem's anatomically precise shoulders, suffused Len with pride. What was Judaism if not an exacting, totalized system of laws handed down by the divine, then kitted out with redundancies and fail-safes by the scholars to eliminate any chance of an infraction—building a wall around the Torah, it was called, the process by which *don't cook a goat in its mother's milk* ballooned into *never mix dairy with meat, buy two sets of dishes, wash them in different dishwashers*—and then, finally, poked full of loopholes so the devout might obediently circumvent those laws?

Len finished his work, sat back on his haunches, rolled his aching neck, and waited.

Five minutes passed, and nothing happened. Len reminded himself that he didn't actually expect anything to, and not because the dirt was improperly sourced or his penmanship was suspect, but because he didn't believe in any of this shit. He stood, dusted himself off, and went inside to grab a beer and text Waleed, see if he was in the neighborhood.

He drank the neck off his beer and thought about the obscurely revolting phrase *drank the neck off his beer,* as he did every single time he drank a beer because he'd once read a hacky detective novel that employed it whenever a character drank a beer, and everybody in that book was an alcoholic.

He drank the chest and stomach off his beer, then startled when he heard a noise outside that sounded like a monster pounding a granite fist against a tiled Moroccan table and smashing it to smithereens.

Len deposited his beer in the sink just as The Golem ripped his back door off the hinges and flung it aside.

"Holy shit," said Len, as The Golem ducked into the apartment and lurched toward him. And all at once, Len realized that while he had been careful to make sure the bottoms of his golem's feet were perfectly aligned, he had neglected to really think about where each leg began, how it fused into the hip, and the result of this negligence was a pronounced limp, perhaps even a dysplasia.

The Golem galumphed to a stop in front of Len, and a pair of eyeballs pushed forward through the milky vacancy of his sockets, like the answer cube floating to the surface of a Magic 8 Ball.

The Golem closed his eyes. Len did not remember providing him with eyelids.

When he opened them, the eyeballs had anchored themselves. The Golem's ink-black pupils dilated, and he seemed to take Len's measure.

"Hi," said Len, stifling a surge of panic. "I, uh . . . I made you."

The Golem's brow furrowed and roiled.

"I'm not really a sculptor," said Len, as the panic softened into self-reproach. "I had some trouble with—"

The Golem wrapped his misshapen hand around Len's neck/shoulder region, his fingers so large—so disproportionately large, Len admonished himself—and so lacking in fine motor skills that it was unclear whether his intention was to choke Len or merely brace him against the wall.

"Vu zaynen mir? Ir zet nit oys vi a rov. Vi lang iz es geven? Ver zol ikh oyshargenen?" demanded The Golem, his voice sludgy, his tongue and vocal cords and trachea and epiglottis nonexistent to the best of Len's knowledge.

"Ver zol ikh oyshargenen?" he said again. Len could tell it was a question by the way The Golem's voice lilted into a slightly less guttural register on the final syllable, and he could tell The Golem really wanted to know the answer by the way he tightened his left-handed vise grip on Len's neck/shoulder and with his right hand punched a massive hole straight through the door of Len's stainless steel refrigerator.

"I'm sorry," said Len. "I don't speak . . . Yiddish?" It was a guess, which Len hoped he could convey by lilting his voice into a slightly higher register despite the increasing pressure The Golem was exerting against his windpipe.

The Golem grunted and flung Len aside, much as he had the door. Len scuttled back against a wall and sat there, panting.

"Thank you," he said after a moment.

The Golem turned away and began to inspect his own body, while Len weighed the idea of trying to download a Yiddish-English voice translation app against the likelihood that if he tried, The Golem would pulverize his phone.

"Avu iz mayn shmok?" The Golem said, without looking up. There was a catch in his voice, as if he were confronting the unthinkable.

An idea struck Len, and he stood and backed into the living room.

The Golem's head whipped toward him with big-carnivore energy, and Len froze and showed The Golem both his palms. "Listen," he said, "I'm going to run out and find someone who can understand you. But I need you to stay here and not trash my place, okay? Can you do that?"

The Golem didn't respond, but he also didn't destroy anything. Len darted over to the television and turned it on.

"Here," he said. "Watch this until I get back." He pointed at the sixty-inch screen, which was filled with Larry David's face.

The Golem took a cautious step forward. He seemed frightened, but entranced. He took another step, and the light from the television bathed his steak of a face.

The Golem blinked, and planted his cinderblock feet.

Len grabbed his keys and bolted for the door.

4

#RealBodegaCat

The bodega cat's name was Adofo, although he hated what that term had come to represent. Typical New Brooklyn bullshit—these people moved here from their windswept cultural wastelands and started fetishizing all the quotidia New Yorkers took for granted, pointing their iPhone cameras at whatever drabs of grit and quirk the city had left and turning it all to kitsch.

For the first fifteen years of his life, nobody had paid Adofo the slightest mind. Maybe if he was lying on top of the bread, a custie might say "Yo papi, you think you could move?", but if he pretended to be asleep they usually just bought some Little Debbie Snack Cakes instead.

Now he couldn't get through a single day without some millennial taking a selfie with him so she could tag it #RealBodegaCats or #SpreadLoveIt'sTheBrooklynWay or whatever the fuck. These people deserved death, and if Adofo hadn't been so old and fat he would have sliced every last one of them to ribbons and feasted on their intestines. The Brooklyn way.

The door dinged and Adofo looked up from the stack of four-day-old *New York Post*s on which he was lounging to see goofy-ass Len Bronstein step inside, the sweat stains beneath the arms of his T-shirt nearly fused to the one spread across its chest, like continents trying to reform Pangaea. Motherfucker was probably stoned as usual. Good for him. Adofo couldn't even remember the last time Farug and Basam, the twin brothers who owned this place, had hit him off with any catnip. Like he had anything better to do than get blazed out of his skull and watch the block gentrify and the world burn. Those dickheads had a lot of nerve, naming him after their Dominican coke connect and then letting him languish, sober as a fucking labradoodle.

Bronstein beelined for Miri, at the counter—the lone woman and the sole non-Yemeni the twins employed, not to mention the only person who ever bothered to freshen Adofo's water or hook him up with a handful of plantain chips or a five-hour energy drink. She never tried to pet him, either; they had a mutual respect thing going on. But that didn't mean Adofo didn't peep her steez. He compiled jackets on all the workers, out of sheer fucking boredom, and Miri was the most intriguing of them all—with the possible exception of Zahid (2017–2020), who jacked off into an empty Doritos bag as many as four times during each eight-hour shift, always while watching old episodes of *Yo! MTV Raps* on his phone, and also ran a scam where he pretended to be a notary public.

To Adofo—and what did he know, he was just a fucking cat—Miri seemed like she was perpetually figuring out how to be normal, or playing catch-up from five seconds behind because she was too distracted by something looming and horrible to really pay attention. There was often a tiny envelope of silence before she spoke, like she was double-checking her words first—even when the conversation was a mundane one, as ninety-nine percent of custie-counter exchanges were. She rocked the same gray cardigan almost every day, and watched reality TV shows with rapt focus, as if she were an extraterrestrial cramming to pass as a native of this stupid planet. She lived in the single room upstairs, which Farug and Basam only rented to employees because you had to use the bathroom in the back of the bodega, full of dirty mops and stacked cases of Arizona Iced Tea.

"Hey," said Bronstein. "You speak Yiddish, right?"

Miri didn't answer right away.

This was the other one percent. Adofo hopped down off the stack of newspapers.

"Sorry. I was in here one time and these two Hasidic kids tried to buy cigarettes, and you, like . . . I dunno, because I don't speak Yiddish, but it seemed like you cursed them out or something, and you definitely didn't sell to them, and they fucking took off running, practically."

Adofo's eyes widened. How had he slept through that?

"I speak Yiddish," Miri said, at last. "I grew up—"

The envelope of silence came midsentence this time.

"I speak Yiddish," she finished.

"Cool, cool," said Bronstein, as if she'd asked him to reverse-describe himself in two words. "So, I've kind of got this situation. It's— I need a translator. At my place. Like eight blocks away."

Miri stepped all the way back from the counter.

Better tighten it up, bro, Adofo thought.

"Sorry, this is coming out weird. I just— I need some help. I'll pay you for your time."

Miri grabbed the cordless phone.

"Please leave," she said.

"It's my grandfather," Bronstein explained. "He hit his head, and now he's only speaking Yiddish. I just want to calm him down."

"So call a doctor."

"Do you know one who speaks Yiddish?"

Miri hesitated for a moment, then said, "I can't leave the store. But if you bring him here, I'll try to help."

Bronstein's eyes flicked left, right, left.

Liar, Adofo thought.

"Avu iz mayn shmok," he blurted. "What does that mean?"

Miri stared at Bronstein for a long time, then said, "It means *Where is my dick*."

"Oh. Shit," said Bronstein, as if this made perfect sense.

Miri narrowed her eyes just slightly, her most catlike and thus most attractive move. "Where *is* his dick?" she asked.

"He's not really my grandfather," said Bronstein. Adofo could see his right hand fisting and unfisting rapidly at his side. "He's a golem. I didn't know I was supposed to make him a dick. No wonder he's mad."

"A golem," Miri repeated.

Adofo didn't know what that meant, but the way she said

it—so inflectionlessly that it was somehow all inflection—made him feel certain that Miri was going to walk off into the night with this damp, untruthful stranger.

He couldn't let that happen. He had to warn her.

Adofo meowed at the top of his lungs, then brushed past Bronstein, summoned all the hops he had left, and leapt onto the counter, four feet off the ground, something he hadn't done since the Bloomberg years.

Miri ignored him, followed Bronstein out the door, and locked it behind her.

So Adofo did the only thing he could. He took a nap.

5

Chances

What were the chances Miri would get fired for shuttering the shop six hours early on a perfect early-summer Saturday night, the streets teeming with hipsters in need of beer, snacks, rolling papers, cat selfies?

Sixteen percent, rising to ninety if Farug and Basam happened to swing by.

What were the chances this guy—Len Bronstein, he'd said his name was, pivoting to face Miri and jutting a clay-encrusted hand at her to shake as soon as she'd finished pulling the metal grate down over the door—had concocted this story about making a golem and needing a translator, and memorized *Where is my dick* in Yiddish and smeared clay on his face and arms and neck in an elaborate ploy to lure her back to his apartment for some rape and murder?

Less than one percent, Miri told herself, as they began to walk. It was an unreasonable level of narrative complexity.

What were the chances anybody would come looking for her if she was wrong?

Also less than one percent.

How much of her childhood had Miriam Apfelbaum spent fantasizing about a golem trudging up out of the East River and tearing a hole in the invisible bubble that enclosed the world of the Sassov Hasidim, smashing its fists through the windows of wig shops and glatt butchers, hurling yeshiva buses off of overpasses, picking up Shomrim and smashing their heads together—a one-man liberation army wreaking so much havoc that Miri could just stroll her little gay ass out of there, unnoticed by one and all?

Maybe eight percent. That was a lot of hours.

What percentage of the Sassov community was gay?

Presumably the same number as the rest of the population. Ten, twelve.

How many of them kept it a secret, or never even figured it out themselves, got married at eighteen to whomever the family and the shadchan agreed on, and started having babies?

One hundred percent, minus Miri.

Was it weird to run away from everyone you had and everything you knew and start over less than a mile away, just outside the meniscus of the bubble, so close you could still hear the mechanical sirens blaring from the yeshivas on Friday afternoons, heralding the coming of the Sabbath?

One hundred percent. But Miri was a New Yorker. What was she supposed to do, move to Ohio? With what money?

Did the existence of a golem imply the existence of God?

One hundred percent. But this was an easy answer, as the existence of bees also implied the existence of God. The existence of existence implied the existence of God. But outside the bubble, beliefs could easily get decoupled from deeds, and if you didn't do *everything*, it became easier and easier to do *nothing*.

This was the brilliance of the world the Hasidim had built. Every moment was accounted for, every decision prescribed, every act an act of devotion.

Miri's first years on her own had not felt like freedom; they had felt like chaos.

"I really appreciate this," Len Bronstein said, hustling her along. The night was warm, the air friendly against Miri's skin.

"You could have taken a video," she said.

Len blinked. "Sorry. What?"

"You could have taken a video of the golem with your phone. To convince me that you were telling the truth."

"I didn't think of that," said Len. "That's really smart." He paused, then added, "I'm an art teacher," for no reason Miri could discern.

"I guess I'm here anyway," she said. They reached the corner, and as they waited for the light to change, a distinctively long-faced character actor stepped out of a New Orleans–themed bar, lit a cigarette, and whipped out his phone.

Miri gasped and grabbed Len's arm, then realized what she'd done and let it go.

"That guy," she said, low, pointing at him with her forehead. "I've seen him in something. A movie. Or a TV show." Why this excited and flummoxed her, Miri could not be sure. There was a sheen of the impossible to the actor, even though he was standing ten feet away; Miri knew he was a real human being, but a part of her refused to believe it, because she had seen him in *that thing*. Then again, the fact that she was no longer a Sassov seemed impossible, too; the fact that she could use her phone to find a woman to date at any time of day or night was utterly absurd. At this very moment, she was risking both her job and her well-being to find out if this strange man had made a golem, and that seemed perfectly reasonable. The only sensible conclusion, Miri decided, was that she was a terrible judge of reality.

"What *was* it?" she muttered, unable to look away. The actor dragged his thumb across his phone, just like a regular person. Miri felt, obscurely, that she ought to do something. But that was asinine.

"Yo, excuse me," Len called, and Miri's stomach lurched. She grabbed his arm again, but it was too late: he was doing it. "I saw you in something, right?"

The actor pointed at Len with his cigarette. "Nah. I saw *you* in something. You was on that show. On NBC. About the cop."

Miri had never heard Len's real laugh, but she could tell the one he laughed now wasn't it. "Come on, man," he said. "I know I saw you in something." He flicked a finger back and forth, at Miri and himself. "We both did."

"It was your mother's cunt," the actor said. He dropped the cigarette, swiped his boot across it, walked to the curb, and opened the back door of an idling black Cadillac Escalade.

"Asshole," said Len, once he'd slammed the door.

"Why did you do that?"

"What? If I was an actor, and somebody cared enough to ask me that question, I'd be fucking flattered. Like it's some great burden, that somebody recognizes you? For your work? Why'd you become an actor, then?"

The light changed, and Len charged into the intersection. Miri followed automatically, replaying the interaction in her head, trying to unwind its strands.

"I pay your fuckin' salary," Len said out of nowhere, presumably to the character actor.

Miri tried to find some way to construe this as anything but nonsense, and could not. Why was she following this man to his apartment again?

Miri stopped walking right in the middle of the intersection, but Len didn't notice and the light was about to change, so she hurried to the curb and said, "Wait. Stop."

Len shoved his hands into the pockets of his jeans. "What?"

"The golem. He doesn't speak Hebrew?"

"I don't know."

"You didn't try?"

"I don't speak Hebrew."

"Then how—"

"It's all on the internet."

The question she was about to ask sent a shudder of terror through Miri's body that she could not begin to understand.

"Are you even Jewish?"

"I'm culturally Jewish."

"I don't know what that means," Miri said, beginning to panic.

"I mean, yes, I'm Jewish. I have four Jewish grandparents. I was bar mitzvahed, sort of."

"What does that mean, sort of?"

"Well, it wasn't— My parents didn't belong to a synagogue, so it was through this Jewish Sunday school I went to. They gave you a choice between learning a Torah portion in Hebrew or giving a speech about a Jewish concept. My boy Jared did his on golems. That was the first time I heard of them. I did mine on tikkun olam. Repairing the world."

"I know what tikkun olam means," Miri said, and if Len noticed that her pronunciation was a repudiation of his, he didn't let on. She swallowed hard. "So? Are you doing it?"

Len picked at the clay stuck in his arm hair, and appeared to give the question some thought. "Well," he said, after a moment, "I know every single person on my block."

"How is that repairing the world?"

"How many people in this city actually know their neighbors?"

Miri thought about the massive building she grew up in. The Sassov families, she knew by name. The others were just others; they'd never exchanged a word.

"I don't know," she said.

"You gotta start somewhere. You gotta repair it a block at a time."

"Right."

He cocked his head at her with a kind of benign curiosity that, to Miri's astonishment, instantly caused her central nervous system to cease its wartime production of adrenaline, epinephrine, and cortisol.

"I take it you're pretty religious?"

"It depends who you ask."

"What if I ask you?"

"I'd say I'm religious."

"And why would I ask anybody else?"

It was, Miri realized, a good question.

"I guess I'm mostly trying to repair myself," she said, and immediately regretted it.

"Nothing wrong with that," announced the newly coronated king of tikkun olam. "Hyperlocal."

They turned onto a wide one-way street of three-story brick row houses and brownstones, and Len pointed one out.

"That's me right there."

It was the prettiest block Miri had ever seen. Of course Len knew all his neighbors. Practically no one lived here.

Heroic Dose

Len pushed his key into the keyhole of his apartment, and the door swung open on its own. A small flower of terror bloomed inside his chest as he imagined The Golem wandering out to roam the streets, not that a locked door would have stopped him. Len's back door, Len reminded himself, was currently lying in the yard, where The Golem had flung it.

"Come on in," he said to Miri, stepping across the threshold. She followed him into the living room.

"Hey, man," said Waleed, from the sofa. "There you are."

The television was still on and *Curb Your Enthusiasm* was still playing, and The Golem was sitting six inches from the screen. His bulbous knees were pressed against his barrel chest and his great lumpy arms hugged them tight, in a grotesque parody of a child who has just snuck downstairs on a Saturday morning to watch cartoons.

Len looked at Miri, and found her glancing back and forth between The Golem—who did not seem to have registered their arrival—and Waleed.

"So, that's The Golem," said Len, pointing at The Golem, "and this is my friend Waleed."

"Hey," said Waleed. "Nice to meet you."

Miri gave him a little wave, and Waleed turned to Len. "I have so many questions," he said.

"Me too," said Len. "Like, what did you do to my golem?"

"Dude," said Waleed. "I walked in, and he grabbed me by my jacket and slammed me against the wall"—Waleed indicated the wall, the plaster cratered so extensively that it was clear to Len that he would never, ever get back his security deposit—"and, like, smelled my head and both my hands."

"Okay," said Len, trying to be patient. Suddenly, he remembered Miri, and the fact that she was a guest here. "Can I get you a drink or something?" he asked.

"No, thank you," Miri said absently. She had ventured quite close to The Golem, and didn't seem to be paying much attention to the conversation. Len thought perhaps he should caution her to back off, but The Golem still hadn't moved.

"Then he tore open my bag," Waleed continued, "and smashed all my cookies and broke my vial of liquid acid, and it, like, absorbed into his body."

Len walked over to the opposite side of The Golem from Miri, and found a vantage point from which he could look down into the creature's eyes. The black pupils had spread like punctured egg yolks, to the very rims of his irises.

Len walked back to Waleed. "How much acid was in the vial?" he asked.

"A hundred milligrams."

"I don't know what that means," said Len. "I'm an American."

"That's a hundred thousand micrograms," Waleed explained.

Len felt himself swell with what he imagined was a Golem-like rage. "If you try to tell me how many deciliters it is," he said, "I will murder you." He pointed at The Golem. "How fucking high is he?"

"I have no idea," said Waleed. "I don't know anything about his body composition. Or his drug history. Or his psychological state. Or what the fuck he is."

"I made him out of clay," said Len.

Waleed considered that for a moment, then said, "That's one big fucking dreidel."

He ran a hand down his beard, then whipped off his wire-rimmed glasses and polished them with a cloth he kept in his pocket. "A recreational dose is about a hundred micrograms. What they call a heroic dose—in, like, the Joseph Campbell sense of the hero's journey, where you face demons and experience ego death and rebirth and shit like that—starts around two hundred."

Len did some quick math in his head.

"And The Golem took fifty times that?"

"Fifty thousand. But we don't— It might not have even crossed the blood-brain barrier."

Miri reached out and poked The Golem in the shoulder, leaving a minute indent in his clay, his flesh, that disappeared after a moment.

"He doesn't have blood or a brain, Waleed."

Waleed patted himself down until he located the slim silver cigarette case in the inside pocket of his blazer. He popped it open, selected an expertly rolled joint, and waved it like a conductor's baton.

"It's a question of having the right neuroreceptors to process entheogens. When our ancestors started taking psilocybin mushrooms about forty thousand years ago, our brains basically rewired themselves, and then we rewired society." He wagged a finger and smiled. "But we had to have those neuroreceptors already, right? So did we use the plants, or did the plants use us?" He lit the joint. "Did I ever pitch you my dolphin LSD handjob movie?"

Miri plopped herself down beside The Golem, her shoulder touching his forearm, and began to watch TV.

"Not that I recall," said Len.

"Oh," said Waleed, "you'd recall. So: It's the late sixties, and the thinking among biologists is that brain-to-body ratio is determinative of intelligence. And dolphins have the highest brain-to-body ratio of any primate."

"I don't think dolphins are primates," said Len.

"Any mammal, then. And this one researcher from Harvard becomes obsessed with teaching them to speak English. He believes they're just as smart as we are, if not smarter, and they already have a complex language, so they should be able to learn ours. He even writes a novel set in the near future where dolphins have a seat on the UN Security Council and shit. And he gets a grant to go set up shop someplace in Hawaii and give it a shot. This all really happened."

Len found his attention waning and glanced over at Miri and The Golem. "I feel like we should do something," he said.

"Let the medicine do its work," Waleed replied, and passed him the joint.

Len took a toke, and Waleed resumed.

"One day, this young woman shows up at the dolphin research center. She's like, *I heard you were here, and I love animals, and I'd just like to help out however I can.* So he gives her a job, and pretty soon it becomes clear that even though she has no scientific training, she's just naturally good with the dolphins, better than any of the grad students or whatever. But it's still slow going, and after a few months she goes to the Harvard guy and tells him she doesn't think she can really make progress just working a few hours a day. She feels like it needs to be much more immersive.

"He's like, *Word.* So they take a house and flood it with water to a depth of like four feet, and she moves into it with this adolescent male dolphin who's the most promising student. She sleeps on a raised platform bed above the water, but otherwise she's just wading around, hanging out with the dolphin. I've seen photos of the house, dude. It's insane. And the idea is that the dolphin is gonna start seeing her as a maternal figure, and his progress is gonna skyrocket.

"And they do this shit for months. But gradually it becomes clear that this dolphin is mad distracted from his studies, because he's going through puberty, and he's super horny, and he doesn't see her as a mother, he sees her as basically his girlfriend who he lives in a house with. So she goes to the Harvard guy like, *Listen, this dude can't pay attention, and I'm thinking maybe I should try to relieve his sexual tension by giving him handjobs.*"

"Get the fuck outta here," said Len. He turned to see if Miri was listening, and found her immobile, deep into whatever unspoken thing she and The Golem were maybe sharing.

"So the scientist is like, *Yup, yup, seems right*. And she starts giving the dolphin handjobs every other day or whatever."

"The water must have gotten so nasty," said Len, and passed Waleed the joint.

"Meanwhile, tons of scientists are getting interested in psychedelics, especially at Harvard. And naturally, this guy decides they should start dosing the dolphins with LSD. So now this motherfucker is living in a house, getting handjobs on a regular basis, and tripping his balls off on acid."

Waleed paused, which was fortunate because Len needed a moment to process all this.

"But like I said, they couldn't tell whether the acid was crossing the blood-brain barrier. And then eventually, some other scientists show up to visit and see what type of utter fucking madness is unfolding at this research station, and they're like *Oh, hell no,* and everything gets shut down. They drain the water house, and the woman leaves. I think somehow the scientist kept his job. But the dolphin is so depressed now that—dolphins are voluntary breathers, right? And this dude decides not to breath. He basically kills himself."

"You can't end a movie like that," said Len.

"Well, here's the kicker. Years and years later, the woman moves back into the water house, which is just a regular house now. She and her husband raise three kids there. She said the place was full of beautiful memories."

"I'd watch that, I guess," said Len.

He stared over at The Golem and wondered what was going on inside his head.

7

Thrash, Memory

There has only ever been one golem. He is not made, but remade—no more a new thing than a person awakening from a nap is a new person.

The Golem is a repository of memories. He retains what he has seen, what he has done, to whom he has done it. He remembers why, if anyone ever bothered to explain it to him.

The Golem has napped far more than he has been awake, but he has been awake far more than is generally thought, because by and large, The Golem operates off the books. Even his name is not a name but a sobriquet, a descriptor. It does appear once in the Torah, but not in reference to him; Adam is called a golem, before God fills him with the breath of life. The scholars say it means *unfinished thing*.

The first golem was sculpted by Moses, from the same mixture of sand, clay, and mud the enslaved Jews formed into the bricks they used to build the Great Pyramids. The words and rituals by which the creature might be brought to life—including the invocation of the secret True Name of God—were revealed by the Angel of Death, shortly after the ravages of the Tenth Plague and just before the frenzied rush to depart from the land of bondage.

The Golem guarded over the Israelites, as they fled by running straight toward a large body of water. When Hashem parted the Sea of Reeds, The Golem held off the pursuing legion of Egyptian soldiers, and when Hashem allowed the walls of water to collapse, The Golem alone survived annihilation—emerging on the far banks when the moon was high and kneeling before his maker so that Moses might uninscribe the aleph from his brow and return him to inchoate matter.

Many scholars consider this a crock of shit, and contend that King Solomon, the Jewish tradition's sagest ruler and most powerful mystic—he of the three hundred wives and seven hundred concubines, he of the ring that controlled demons and animals, he who sired the dynastic King Menelik of Ethiopia with Sheba, he upon whose grave the Rastafarians say cannabis plants were found growing, he whose very name remains synonymous with wisdom—was the father of The Golem. That by applying his holy intellect to the highest mysteries of the universe, he was able to learn how to give form to formlessness as none but Adonai had. The Golem of Solomon worked tirelessly to hew and heft the stones that became the central Temple of Jerusalem—Judaism's great seat of spiritual authority and Solomon's signature achievement.

Others call this a fallacy, and hold that the first golem was not created until after Alexander the Great died, and his empire fractured, and the new ruler of Judea, King Antiochus, outlawed the keeping of kashrut law, the ritual of circumcision, the holding of Shabbat services, and all the other laws and customs of the Jews, forcing them to worship the Greek gods on pain of death.

Two years into the reign of Antiochus, a priest named Mattathias ben Yohanan, a descendant of Moses's brother Aaron, happened upon a Hellenist Jew sacrificing at the altar of Apollo. So Mattathias killed him, because it says right in the Ten Commandments that Jews cannot worship any god but Hashem, shortly before it says they must not kill.

Mattathias fled into the mountains with his five sons and was soon joined by other rebels. They formed an army— small, outnumbered, hopeless—to fight both Antiochus's Greek-Syrian army and the Jews who acquiesced in the worship of false gods. It is at this point that Mattathias turned to occultism and created The Golem, to defend the Jews from their most dangerous enemies.

Upon suscitation, The Golem deemed Mattathias's bloodthirsty zealotry to be a greater danger to the Jews than the army of the king, and promptly thrashed him to death. Mattathias's son Judah Maccabee assumed command of the army, winning a three-year guerrilla campaign that is generally yadda-yaddaed in favor of focusing on the fact that afterward, when they cleaned up the Temple, the 164 BCE equivalent of a lightbulb outlasted its warranty. This is because the government Judah founded, the Hasmonean Dynasty, spent the next century oppressing its own people and

playing grab-ass with the Roman Empire, and by the time
the Hanukkah story was set down in the Mishnah, nobody
wanted to make them heroes. Certainly, there was no pre-
dicting such an outcome from the beginning of the story,
when Mattathias murders a fellow Jew merely for obeying a
law the man would have been killed for flouting.

Regardless, it is highly implausible that the Macca-
bees had a golem. Far more likely is that he entered the
historical record sometime in the ensuing few centuries.
With the Hasmoneans in power, the Jewish people were
finally free to form a number of parties that hated each
other, and destroy themselves from within. The most powerful of these was the Sadducees, or Temple Cult, who
labored to make the reconsecrated Temple the be-all and
end-all of Jewish life. Any kosher animal within a hundred
miles of the Temple was at constant risk of being sacrificed
by the Sadducees, and some scholars believe that the high
priest Simeon created The Golem to act as a kind of eter-
nally vigilant Temple watchman. But this is likely a confla-
tion of the myth of Talos, a bronze robot whom the Greek
god Hephaestus forged to patrol the island of Crete in the
age of King Minos.

The Sadducees' rivals were the Pharisees, who believed
in the Oral Torah given to Moses by Hashem, which later
became the basis for the Talmud. The Pharisees were more
interested in forging personal relationships to God than in
setting goats on fire, and they encouraged Jews to worship
and study Torah privately instead of investing all their time
and money in the Temple and its priests.

Unsurprisingly, this enraged the Temple and its priests,
who induced the Hasmonean rulers to kill thousands of

Pharisees in the years to come—which is why some believe the desperate Pharisees plumbed their sacred teachings and figured out how to make a golem to defend themselves.

This seems unlikely, because if the Pharisees had had a golem, they would not have gotten their asses kicked all up and down the fecund plains of Judea. But they did invent something nearly as useful: a decentralized model of worship and study that would help the Jews survive when everybody else began trying to kill them in the years to come.

The next credible mention of The Golem comes in the fourth century of the Common Era, when the Roman emperor Constantine converted to Christianity, bringing most of his subjects with him. This was unprecedented and astonishing—as if Derek Jeter woke up one day and decided to get a Red Sox logo tattooed across his chest, and then every Yankees fan went out and did the same.

The surgent Christian faith was at great pains to distinguish itself to potential converts—to explain how a religion based on the worship of the Jewish son of the Jewish God was not merely some substrain of Judaism. The simplest and most elegant way to illustrate the differences, it turned out, was to kill as many Jews as possible for the next fifteen hundred years.

Constantine began by passing laws against interfaith marriage and synagogue building, and a rabbi whose name is lost to history, if he existed at all—the Jews had rabbis instead of priests now, because the Temple had been destroyed and you couldn't have a priest without a temple, and the army they sent to fight the Romans had been defeated and marched back to Rome as slaves, and Judea was now called Palestine—conceived of a plot to assassinate Constantine before things got any worse, and crafted a golem out of mud from the banks of the River Tiber to deliver the fatal blow.

This golem, unlike previous golems (if there had been previous golems), took the form of a seductress. Though still male in essence (if he could be said to have either gender or essence), this golem was voluptuously formed, attired in the raiment of a courtesan, and sent to capture the emperor's attention, secure a private audience, and throttle him to death.

The mission ended in failure, and the entire story is patently absurd. The persecution of the Jews ramped up, and they fled Palestine for what would surely be easy times in Italy, Spain, and Germany.

LOL.

These early golem tales are probably apocryphal; the true age of the golem began a few hundred years after Constantine, when the slaughter of Jews shifted temporarily from a state-mandated, state-funded, state-staffed activity to a spontaneous, sporting act of private enterprise that was heartily endorsed by the state. The Crusades are usually thought of as Christian holy wars carried out to reclaim Palestine by killing or converting the Muslims who now controlled it. But most crusades kicked off with a festive, informal warm-up massacre of the local Jewish population. The fact that Jews were not allowed to own weapons made these pogroms perfect low-stakes team-building opportunities.

The provocation was often one of two gluten-related falsehoods: the Blood Libel or the Desecration of the Host. The former was the claim that matzoh was made with the blood of Christian babies (asking how the Jews made mat-zoh for three thousand years before there *were* any Christian babies could also get you killed); the latter was the accusation that Jews had broken into a church and stuck pins in the Communion wafers in order to torment Jesus (although any such Jews would have considered those wafers to be merely wafers, as Jews do not believe in transubstantiation).

These were unpredictable centuries for the diasporic Jews of Europe; one moment you were simply a regular citizen who paid higher taxes and was not allowed to own land or weapons or ride a horse, and the next a mob was coursing through the capillaries of the village, burning down your home and murdering your children in the street.

In the face of such horror and defenselessness, tales of The Golem proliferated as never before.

He patrolled Prague's Jewish Quarter every night for months, until calls for the expulsion of the Jews were somehow quelled.

In Lithuania, he kept a mob at bay after a Christian child fell down a well and drowned, supposedly as a result of a Jewish hex.

He served the Grand Rebbe of Odessa for decades, traveling with him from synagogue to synagogue across the perilous countryside—but was always immobilized from Friday sundown to Saturday sundown, lest he desecrate the Sabbath.

The Golem of Lublin never stopped growing; he rampaged about laying waste to buildings and devouring livestock until his head touched the very heavens; a local idiot saved the town by lulling him into somnolence with a long and pointless story so the rabbi could approach on the back of a donkey and perform the unmaking.

The Golem of Bremen paddled a massive wooden raft across a flood-swollen river, saving the Jews from a pogrom, then disappeared beneath the water forever.

The Golem of Vienna was instructed to stand watch over the synagogue during the High Holidays, but he fell in love with a Christian girl and followed her home, allowing the congregation to be trapped inside and burned to death.

In 1391, a wave of violence led many Spanish Jews to convert to Christianity—or did they? Perhaps, thought the wily Queen Isabella, they were secretly still practicing their religion, so quietly and harmlessly that it was impossible to tell. Her solution to this vexing conundrum was the Spanish Inquisition, which entailed investigating every single converso by means of a secret police force operated by the Catholic Church, seizing the children of anyone found to still be Jewish and handing them over to be raised by monks and nuns, then torturing the adults until they confessed.

The rest of Europe, bearing witness to this systematic barbarism, decided it looked like tremendous fun and joined right in.

The Golem whose legend spread during these years specialized in rescuing Jewish children from monasteries—sometimes posing as a monk himself, beneath a cowl and behind a vow of silence—and transporting them to a hidden cave, where he sustained them on the meat he hunted, and in some tellings captured and tamed a she-bear whom he tasked with raising them.

It is difficult to reconcile this iteration of The Golem, clever and subtle, more spy than soldier, with any previous one. But then, there is little that remains consistent among the disparate legends of The Golem, and very little reason to put much stock in the veracity of any of them.

In September 1941, thirty-three thousand seven hundred and seventy-one Jews were shot to death by German soldiers in Kyiv, Ukraine, over a thirty-six-hour period. Their bodies were cast into a ravine called Babyn Yar, which was more than a hundred feet deep and a quarter mile long. Rumor has it that The Golem was among them. It is the last time he appears in the folklore of the Jewish people.

8

Where Is Crisis?

"Why The Golem here?"

Len opened his eyes and found that it was morning. He did not remember falling asleep. Standing before him was The Golem, hunched beneath a ceiling scarcely higher than his head.

"You speak English?"

"The Golem learn."

Len looked past him and saw Miri sprawled out on the rug, snoring raggedly, surrounded by jagged bits of broken screen. At the center of Len's television was a massive, fist-shaped black hole that appeared to be sucking a spiderweb of glass into its field of gravity.

"Why'd you break my TV?" asked Len.

"Because get furious when funny Jew go away." His accent was definitely Eastern European, every consonant a glottal mess or a scythe.

Miri stirred at the sound of his voice, and sat up.

"He speaks English," Len reported. He stood, and peered up into The Golem's eyes. "How was your trip? Did you trip? It seemed like you were tripping hard, but I mean, I don't really know you well enough to say."

For a moment, The Golem was silent. Then, "The Golem relive past," he said with a grimace. "Never do that before." He shook his massive head. "Shit is horrible."

"What past?" said Miri, padding over in her socks. "He just made you."

"The Golem stay The Golem," said The Golem.

Miri narrowed her eyes. "So you were the Golem of Prague? Of Chelm?"

"Prague. Chelm story not real."

"Egypt?" Len asked.

"Think so," said The Golem. "But The Golem not have time to play game of what is real." He tapped Len on the chest with a granite-hard forefinger. "Why The Golem here? And where The Golem's dick? You say dick, or cock?" He nodded at the television. "He say both."

"Dick is probably better," said Len. "Cock is kind of porny. I'm sorry, I didn't know I was supposed to make you one. And I think it's probably too late now."

The Golem roared, grabbed Len by the shoulder, and pitched him sideways. Len flew into the arm of the couch, flipped ass over teakettle, and landed in a heap on the floor.

"Hey!" said Miri, and The Golem whirled toward her, eyes pinprick-focused, nostrils flared.

She was uncowed. "That's unnecessary. He did the best he could."

Len stood and brushed himself off.

"Make your own dick," he said. "Give yourself an asshole too."

The Golem threw him a dark look, but it was a look of resignation—a look that said he understood the dick ship had sailed. "You rabbi or priest?"

"Neither."

The Golem arched an eyebrow as thick as a bistro filet, then screwed up his lips, trying to come up with the word. He couldn't. He looked to Miri. "Novi."

"Prophet," she translated.

"I'm not a prophet. I'm just some schmuck. I was fucking around."

The Golem lumbered closer. "The Golem is for time of Jewish crisis. Where is crisis?"

Len blinked, sat down, and gave this some thought.

"There's a lot of handwringing about intermarriage," he said. "Israel-Palestine is a fucking shit show. Most people try not to bring it up. Um . . . I know more and more Jewish couples who definitely do not want to circumcise if they have boys, but a lot of times their parents—"

"Do not be putz!" thundered The Golem, and pushed the couch onto its back with his foot.

Len rolled off and sprung back up. "Fine. Come here, then. Gimme your forehead. I'll turn you back to clay."

The Golem covered it with both his hands and shook his head slowly. "Something not right. Hashem would not let—"

He winced, and looked again to Miri. "What is word. Moyshe kapoyer. Shoyte ben pikholts."

"Um . . . Moses backward-ass. Complete idiot."

Len crossed his arms. "Ass-backward, not backward-ass."

The Golem nodded, and resumed.

"Hashem would not let not-priest, not-rabbi, not-prophet ass-backward idiot to make The Golem without reason."

"Or maybe you're not as fuckin' important as you think," said Len. "Or, here's a reason. Paying me back for my door, and my wall, and my TV. There's your reason." Even as he said it, he knew it made no sense, and that Miri and probably The Golem would know it made no sense.

The Golem ignored him—which felt like charity, which felt worse than being insulted—and turned to Miri.

"Who trying to kill Jews?" He spun in a circle. "What country we in?" The Golem narrowed his eyes. "Feel like maybe Prussia, if The Golem have to guess."

"It's America," said Len. "And nobody is trying to kill us."

"America," repeated The Golem. He looked around the room as if seeing it for the first time. "Heard good things. Mostly in middle of pogrom. People say America might help with problem of—"

The Golem's English failed him, and he pounded his left fist into his right hand. "Dos kleyne dayshishe shtik drek mit di shlimazeldike vontses. Yes?"

Miri looked like she was going to throw up.

"I need to speak to you outside," she said to Len.

Things Always Bad

"'That little German piece of shit with the stupid mustache,'" Miri said, the second they stepped outside. The block was far warmer than Len's apartment. Or maybe she was just having a panic attack. "That's what he said."

She waited for Len to get it, but he didn't, so she told him.

"He doesn't know about the Holocaust." She looked at Len's door and felt a hot tear leak from her eye. "We have to tell him."

He studied her a moment—long enough for Miri to wonder whether she was wrong, then chastise herself for allowing a bone-deep conviction to be upended by the arched eyebrow of a shmegegge.

"Do we, though?" said Len.

"His whole life—"

"Life," Len repeated, waggling the top two knuckles of both index and middle fingers as if he were scratching the air. Miri had no idea what this meant, or why it was worth interrupting her for.

She started again.

"His whole life, he's defended us. He can't *not know*."

"Know what?" asked Waleed, strolling up the block with a cardboard drink-holder balanced atop his palm. "I got us coffee." He pried the cups free and distributed them.

"Know about the Holocaust," said Len. "Apparently, he doesn't."

Waleed sipped his coffee, blinked, and nodded. "Yeah. You've gotta tell him."

"Okay," said Len, "but I'm warning you, he's not gonna like it."

Miri just stared at him, her face throwing off so much heat she expected to see the air between the two of them go wavy.

"You know what I mean." Len took the lid off his coffee and peered into the steaming liquid, then tried to reattach it and bent the rim of the cup and cursed.

Miri took a deep breath, turned on her heel, and stalked back inside.

The Golem was precisely as she had left him, gazing at the spot where Miri had last stood. She thought of her laptop, the way it spun down into power-saving mode when it detected disuse. Did The Golem have an interior life, a voice inside his head? Or did he merely stand fallow until there was something to react to?

Was an inner voice the same thing as a soul?

Miri resumed her previous position.

"What's the last thing you remember, before this?" she asked. "Before America?"

The Golem told her about the soldiers, the ravine, and blackness.

Miri felt her heartbeat quicken. She sat down on the closest available surface, which happened to be the floor.

This was a story she knew, a story she had always known.

Among the thirty-three thousand seven hundred and seventy-one Jews murdered and cast into Babyn Yar had been Grand Rebbe Yehuda Sassov, the third man to lead the Sassov Hasidim since the community's founding in 1764 by Yehuda's grandfather Zalman Sassov.

Joining the Grand Rebbe in death were his son and anointed successor, Yissichar, Yissichar's wife, Alona, and five of their six children. The Rebbe's four daughters and their husbands and his other twenty grandchildren had fled six months earlier, but Yehuda and Yissichar were intent on remaining in Kyiv until they could leave with the last of their people. They ministered to the women, the children, and the elderly, the Jews too poor or sick or young or old to travel, the men unfit to be conscripted into the Red Army.

And instead of leaving with the last of their people, Yehuda and Yissichar died with them.

Nor did any of Yehuda's daughters or their children escape Europe, or survive the war.

But the Sassov dynasty endured.

Over the course of that day and a half on which thirty-three thousand seven hundred and seventy-one Jews were executed, twenty-five survived. One was Menachem Sassov, the seven-year-old grandson of the Grand Rebbe. The bullet fired at the back of his small skull went wide and hit the woman atop whom Menachem had been ordered to lie, a woman killed an hour earlier.

He hid among and then beneath the bodies, breathing in death and reciting the words of the Sh'ma, for as long as he could bear.

Then Menachem climbed out of the pit and ran into the woods, away from the sound of violins and the smell of roasted meat; it was government policy for the soldiers to host an evening of eating, drinking, and revelry after each mass killing, to bolster the spirits of the townsfolk.

Four months later, Menachem Sassov was smuggled into Switzerland like hope itself, with his head uncovered and his payos shorn, and from there he made his way to Palestine, where the Sassov community numbered eleven households.

Eighty-one years later, Grand Rebbe Menachem Sassov lived one point three miles from Miri's apartment, in what had once been a trio of double-wide brownstones and was now a single residence that served as the headquarters, nerve center, and royal palace of the hundred-thousand-member Sassov community.

Miri had never set foot there. She had grown up with her parents and her seven siblings in a three-bedroom apartment in the Taylor Wythe Houses, shoulder to shoulder with poor Sassov families just like hers—so many that they easily filled the building's racial equity quota for white tenants, so many that the elevators were programmed to stop on every floor from Friday afternoon to Saturday night lest the Sassovs have to climb the stairs or speak to the neighbors.

So many, packed together so tightly in so many buildings just like hers, that the Grand Rebbe controlled a voting bloc large enough to swing any election, which was how the Sassovs had amassed the political power to maintain their own police force, their own ambulance service, their own schools, their own system of justice.

The story of Menachem's survival was the creation myth of Miri's people, and now there was another chapter.

"In Kyiv," said Miri. "Who made you? The Grand Rebbe?"

The Golem nodded.

"Do you remember his family? His grandchildren?"

The Golem nodded again. "They all dead. The Golem fail."

"Not everybody," said Miri, with a surge of happiness so intense and unexpected that it brought tears to her eyes for the second time in ten minutes. "The youngest grandson lived. He's here. He became the Grand Rebbe. The Admor."

The clumsy, monochromatic planes of The Golem's face arranged themselves into an expression of astonishment.

"The Golem need see him," he said.

"I don't— I can't— I'm not the one to make that happen."

Miri remembered that she'd recently been in possession of a coffee, and now she found it in her hand and guzzled some down. Waleed had doctored it with heavy cream and a massive amount of sugar, which struck her as an extreme thing to do to a stranger's drink. But Waleed also seemed like the kind of person who would prepare yours the way he liked his.

Miri felt her blood sugar spike, the caffeine sluice through her brain. She needed all of it right now.

"I have to tell you something," she said. "After you failed. After Babyn Yar. Things . . . got bad."

"Things always bad," The Golem said.

"The Nazis killed six million Jews."

The Golem sat down hard on the couch, which broke beneath his weight. The Golem didn't seem to notice.

"How?" he asked.

Miri thought about how to answer that, whether to talk about laws or trains or camps or gas. Finally, she spoke just one word.

"Efficiently."

The Golem cradled his head in his hands, then balled his hands into fists and gritted his teeth.

"Why nobody make The Golem?" he asked.

It did not seem to Miri like a question that had an answer, so she stayed quiet.

A long time passed before The Golem lifted his head and asked, "How many Jews left?"

"Millions," said Miri, realizing she should have said that up front, framed all this much better. "It's been eighty years. We repopulated."

She flashed on the teeming streets a mile east, awash in Sassovs, Belzers, Bobovers, Lubavitchers, Satmars, Vishnitzers, Klausenbergers, Skverers, Munkaczers, Gerers. Some of the sects were ardent Zionists; others insisted with equal fervor that a Jewish state should not exist until the Messiah showed his face—that if it did, he would not come. And still others believed that he had already come and gone, in the form of their rebbe.

But what united them all, bridged every theological chasm and superseded every political jousting match, was the mandate to have as many children as possible.

Four was unthinkable. Six was lamentable. Eight was average.

Miri had said *we* repopulated, but that was a lie. She had not taken part, except by being born.

"Who knows what percentage Jews make up of the world's population?" Len asked, from behind her. Miri had not noticed him enter. "Go ahead, take a guess."

"One percent," Waleed said, beside him.

"Good try. Miri?"

She was caught between fury at Len's failure to read the room and consternation at the fact that she had no idea what the answer was.

"Two," she said, wanting to outbid Waleed.

"Point one nine," said Len triumphantly. "Less than one fifth of one percent. And it's never been much more. Think about that for a minute. How you gonna blame everything on point one nine percent of the population? We control Hollywood? Politics? The world economy?" He showed them the centimeter of space between his thumb and index finger. "We're *this* big. Fuck happened to my couch?"

The Golem stood.

"The Golem need to see him," he said for the second time, and from the gravel in his voice, Miri understood that The Golem was not going to drop it.

"There might be a way," she said. "But I'm going to hate it."

10

Return of the Shonda

"**P**ark there," said Miri, pointing to a length of curb stenciled AUTHORIZED VEHICLES ONLY. Past it, on the other side of a high fence topped with razor wire, was a large lot, empty save for half a dozen identical black SUVs with tinted windows, bumper guards, police-style siren bars. Behind the lot sat a long two-story brick building that looked—like everything else around here that wasn't new luxury condominiums—as if it used to be a factory. It had those windows Len liked, the kind shaped like upside-down U's.

He obliged, piloting the rented moving van—the largest one available at the U-Haul depot on Atlantic Ave—into the space.

"Authorized Vehicles Only," he read aloud, just to make sure Miri hadn't missed it.

"Classic. What does that even mean? Authorized by who? The city?"

"It doesn't say," Len said, unsure whether these were questions to which Miri knew the answers.

"Exactly." She climbed out of the passenger seat. "Open the back."

Len threw the lock and rolled up the door and there was The Golem, sitting against the rear wall with his hands in his lap, his legs kicked out in front of him. He squinted when the light hit his eyes.

The street was industrial, the signage in Hebrew. Or possibly Yiddish. A yeasty smell floated in the air, so maybe one of these buildings was a bagel factory or something. Bagels had to come from somewhere.

Miri scanned the street and saw no one. "All right," she said. "Let's go."

The Golem earthwormed himself forward, knees to chest, knees to chest, then dipped a leg out of the tailgate as if testing the temperature of a bathtub. Miri pointed at the gate. "Open that, please."

"There's a buzzer," Len pointed out.

"Yes. But we're not going to use it."

The Golem lumbered over, cocked his head sideways as if contemplating the best path forward, then ripped the entire gate loose with one hand and flung it behind him. It pinwheeled through the air, hit the U-Haul at an angle, and shattered the passenger's side window.

"For fuck's sake, The Golem!" Len said. "That was completely unnecessary. Now I have to pay for that."

"You not poor," The Golem replied, and before Len could ask how he'd arrived at that conclusion or how it justified anything, Miri was ushering The Golem back into the van and pulling down the door. And then she was cutting through the lot and Len was scurrying to catch up, like some fucking short-legged asshole child.

She reached the building's giant metal double doors and thumped the heel of her fist against one.

Len heard male voices inside, and then the door swung wide and a young, scowling Hasid faced them. He flicked his eyes up and down Len first, then Miri—assessing them in order of threat potential, Len thought.

"How did you get in here?" he asked, in an English that rolled off his tongue with all the grace of two drunks trying to exit a bar at the same time. The crest on his blue windbreaker looked like a police shield, if you didn't look hard enough, but the letters read SSSP. In tiny writing below that was SASSOV SHOMRIM SAFETY PATROL.

Miri twisted backward and nodded at the gaping hole where the gate had been. "The door was open."

The Hasid looked where she was looking, and unholstered his gun.

"Put up your hands!" he barked.

Len obeyed. Miri jammed hers in her pockets and said, "Is my brother here?"

When he didn't answer, she said it again in Yiddish. Or so Len assumed, because the Hasid said something back that sounded like a question, and then Miri said "Maylekh Apfelbaum," and the Hasid put away his gun.

"I'm Miriam," she continued. "Maybe you've heard of me." From the look on his face, it was clear that he had.

He reached for the back of his belt, unclipped a walkie-talkie, and held Miri's gaze as he spoke into it, in English. At

first Len thought that was for his benefit, but then he realized it was a provocation aimed at Miri. A demotion.

"Maylekh, return to base. Your sister is here."

A burst of static, and then Maylekh must have asked
which sister, because when the Hasid depressed the button
with his thumb and started to answer, Miri spoke over him:

"The shonda. Hurry up. I wouldn't be here if it wasn't
important."

The Hasid stuffed the walkie back where it came from
before Miri could profane it any further. Thirty seconds earlier he'd been threatening to shoot them, and now he looked
like he would crawl inside his own asshole just to get away
from her.

Miri must have noticed too, because she said, "So can
we wait for him inside? You got any rugelach?"

The Hasid goggled at her.

"I'm kidding. We'll wait by the curb. Come on."

She marched up to the van and banged on the side.
"Okay in there?"

The Golem banged back, much harder than he needed
to but perhaps as lightly as he could.

Len sat down on the curb. "Shonda means . . . lesbian?"

Miri snorted. "Shonda is 'shame.' But yes, Len. I'm a
lesbian."

Len nodded, and told himself that silence was okay
sometimes. But he never believed it for long.

"So," he said after a moment. "Family reunion, huh?"

"It's been eight years. I don't even know who he married.
Or how much he blames me for it."

"Why would he blame you for who he married?"

"Right. Why would that make any sense to you." Miri

raked both hands through her hair, and shook it out. "You know our marriages are arranged?"

"I guess I knew that."

"Well, if someone brings shame to your family, it affects your prospects. Like for example if your older sister turns eighteen, rejects every boy they try to match her with for a year, then announces she's gay and leaves the community to go live a life of sin. S'a lebn erger vi a khaye—a life worse than an animal."

Miri stared out at the low-slung skyline for a moment.

"I'm the seventh of eight kids. And Maylekh's only fourteen months younger. I could have waited for him to turn eighteen."

"Could you, though?" asked Len, wanting to exonerate her. "At some point, wouldn't they have made you pick somebody?"

Miri shrugged, but the question seemed to make her feel better. "My parents were already furious."

"The irony," said Len, "is that your brother probably ended up marrying a lesbian."

Miri scowled. "What?"

It had seemed funny in his head.

"Sorry. I just— You said you fucked up his prospects, so I was just thinking, they probably stuck him with somebody else they couldn't marry off."

"Yes," said Miri. "Like an orphan. Or someone who was abused."

"Oh. That's . . . not as funny."

Len startled at the sound of rubber screeching against asphalt, and looked up to see a tinted-out black SUV corner onto the block, then pull up short—presumably at the sight of them.

A dude who could only have been Maylekh Apfelbaum threw open the driver's door and stalked over, legs pumping, arms stiff, nothing above the waist moving at all—cop shit, molded plastic action figure authoritarian shit. And that was even before you noticed the bulk of his bulletproof vest beneath the SSSP windbreaker, or factored in the way he left the car angled across both lanes like he owned the street, engine running as if global warming didn't bother him at all.

God, Len hated cops. And in his whole life, he suddenly realized, he'd maybe never seen a Jewish one.

"What do you want, Miri? Who's this?" She stood, so Len did too.

"Calm down, Maylekh. Say hello."

Maylekh's jaw flared beneath his beard, and he did not say hello.

"It suits you," said Miri, flicking her eyes at the SSSP baseball cap, the heavy boots, the utility belt, the gun. "I wouldn't have thought so, but it does."

"I don't care what you think," Maylekh spat, and Len thought, Yes he does.

"Len Bronstein," he said, extending a hand and then withdrawing it when Maylekh made no attempt to shake.

"Okay then."

Something seemed to shift in Miri's brother as he scrutinized Len.

"You are Jewish?"

"Maybe not compared to you."

"He's not my boyfriend," Miri said, and from the look on Maylekh's face, it seemed that she had read his mind correctly. "That's not what this is."

Maylekh spread his arms, then dropped them to the broad belt, laden with weapons. "So what, then?"

"I need to see the Grand Rebbe."

Maylekh laughed the cruelest laugh Len had ever heard. "You must be on drugs. You are a disgrace in the eyes of Hashem, Miri. In the eyes of your family. The Admor would never see you."

"Well, not me. A friend of mine." Miri turned to Len. "Show him."

Len walked to the van and began rolling up the door. The Golem ducked beneath when it was only halfway raised, in his eagerness to exit.

By the time he straightened to his full height, Maylekh was pointing a gun at him.

"This is The Golem," said Miri. "The Golem, this is my brother Maylekh, who is going to put his gun away now."

But Maylekh did no such thing. Instead, he bent his knees slightly and spread his feet a little wider. A marksman's stance, thought Len.

"Take it easy," he said. "He's a protector of the Jews. Just like you."

Maylekh did not appear to see the similarity. "This thing is a farzeyenish," he said, moving his gun up and down an invisible y-axis, as if deciding whether to place his bullet in the head, the torso, or the knee.

"This monster saved the Admor's life," said Miri.

"That not true," The Golem said. "He save his own life. But The Golem gotta see him." He pointed at Maylekh. "And if you don't stop point that pistol at The Golem, The Golem gonna break in half, then shove both half up your pisshole."

"His English is really impressive," Len whispered to Miri.

Before Maylekh could get off a retort or a shot, The Golem was in motion, moving faster than Len would have believed possible. He closed the distance between them and wrapped his massive fist around the gun and the hand that held it.

He squeezed, and Maylekh cried out and buckled at the knees.

When The Golem unclenched his fist, the gun clattered to the ground in three mangled pieces.

Maylekh cradled his hand against his chest, eyes wide with disbelief and watery with pain.

The Golem looked down at the gun parts and shrugged. "So not half. Threes."

"Thirds," said Len. "Please don't shove them anywhere."

"You boss," The Golem said. He looked at Maylekh. "If The Golem farzeyenish, how come every time The Golem get made it by holy men, huh shit-for-brains?" He looked at Len. "Not this time, but every other time."

Miri knelt beside her brother. "Let me see."

"Fuck off," Maylekh hissed.

"We should take you to the hospital."

"I'll take myself."

Miri lifted his chin so that Maylekh was looking right into her eyes.

"Not if I have The Golem smash your car," she said sweetly. "Now, how about this. Your friend in there, the one who called you, what's his name?"

"Pinchas."

"Tell Pinchas to take us to see the Admor, and you go get that hand looked at. And I promise, I'll leave you alone. Although I'd love to know about your children first. Like how many you have. And with who."

Maylekh glared at her. Then, very slowly, he let go of his injured hand, reached around to the back of his belt, and unclipped his walkie-talkie.

Exodus

Daniel Kempfer had been flipping the same coin for eight years—ever since the day the Admor summoned him to the grand study sprawled across the fourth floor of the house and told Daniel about the plan.

Heads: evolve or die.

Tails: change and die.

If everything went according to plan, they'd find out which in about two years, and the Admor would still be alive to see it.

That part was up to Hashem. The rest was in Daniel's hands.

Menachem had spoken in his usual tone of gentle bemusement that morning—a voice that was a worldview, a voice that never failed to remind Daniel of the first story the Grand Rebbe had ever told him, when he was a fifteen-year-old sheygets from a nothing family with a face stained baby blue and open cuts across his knuckles.

The night before that meeting, he'd been smoking an illicit cigarette with his friend Baruch on Lee Avenue—the street dark, the corrugated metal gates drawn over the doors of hat shops and bakeries—when two shadowy figures rounded the block from Roebling, squared up before the travel agency on the corner, and pulled something from their coat pockets. Daniel heard *clicka-clacka, clicka-clacka, psssht,* and two fat, vivid lines of color arced onto the grate.

He threw down his cigarette and marched across the street.

Are you crazy? Baruch hissed, in Yiddish. *What are you doing?*

If you're scared, go home, Daniel answered, without turning his head. And that was the last he saw of Baruch that night.

One of the vandals heard footsteps, and spun to face the interloper.

Yo, can I help you with something?

Daniel, ensconced in the closed world of the Sassovs, did not register the vandal as Dominican or Italian or Puerto Rican or Polish, the way he would today. He was merely a goy about Daniel's age.

As for the goy, he probably didn't consider the kid who met him at the curb a threat, because Daniel was dressed like an eighteenth-century Ukrainian rabbi.

Daniel answered his question with a question, which was also very rabbinical.

Why don't you destroy your own neighborhood?

Then he hit him with a straight right to the gut, and as the kid doubled forward, Daniel dropped him with a left.

Daniel had five older brothers.

He straddled the kid, lifted him by his lapel, cocked back an arm.

Get off him!

The voice was female. Rabbinically, Daniel ignored it.

A blast of spray paint blinded him, and Daniel released the vandal, sluiced the sticky wetness from his face, and heard the siren.

By the time he could see clearly again, the girl was sprinting away down Roebling, and a couple of Shomrim were stepping out of a car.

One crouched to zip-tie the vandal's hands behind his back, as the other studied Daniel.

Are you all right? the man he would soon come to know as Sol asked, in Yiddish. Daniel nodded, then picked up the can of Krylon at his feet and handed it over.

Sol looked at it, then at the gate of the travel agency, and then he spoke to his partner.

Call the precinct. Tell them we have another hate crime.

He turned back to Daniel.

He attacked you?

This, Daniel had the presence of mind to realize, was the kind of moment upon which an entire future might hinge.

No, he said. *I attacked him.*

The next day, Daniel was sitting on a bench outside Menachem Sassov's famous study. No member of his family had even been invited into this house before.

On the other side of the door, he could hear the Admor's voice.

Perhaps you mistake anger for courage. The work of the Shomrim requires judgment.

The other voice was Sol's: *Judgment, I can teach him.*

The door opened, and Sol beckoned him inside and into a chair.

Before Daniel was a massive desk piled high with gold-leafed tomes, and behind the desk was the Grand Rebbe. His eyes were bright blue, dancing within a filigree of wrinkles.

Give him some tea, he said to Sol, and then he told Daniel a story.

One day, a traveling musician arrives in the town of the Baal Shem Tov and begins to play a wonderful song in the village square. Soon a large crowd has gathered, dancing in the street, spinning and jumping and waving their arms. A deaf man walks by, and stops when he sees the spectacle. Have the people lost their minds, he wonders? Why are they behaving in such a manner?

And the Baal Shem Tov says, *We, the Jewish people, are moved to ecstasy by the melody that issues forth from every creature in the whole of Adonai our God's creation. If this makes us look crazy to people with less sensitive ears, should we not dance?*

The Admor sipped his tea, so Daniel sipped his.

Sol says you love your people, the Admor said. *This is a very fine quality. Some men study the holy books for many years and never find such love.*

Yes, Admor, said Daniel.

There are many ways to be a learned man, said the Admor. And when Daniel stood up from his chair, his training began.

At first he was a blunt instrument, like Sol. But his

anger burned off quickly, and soon it became clear that Hashem had endowed him with other qualities, brought him to the Grand Rebbe's attention for other reasons. Even in a patrol car, Daniel was subtle. His ruthlessness was not that of an enforcer, but a chess master. By the time he was twenty, Daniel was accompanying Menachem to negotiations with real estate developers and city councilmen, his English as fluent as his Yiddish. At twenty-two, he married one of the Admor's granddaughters.

Many times during those years, Daniel thought about the story of the musician and the Baal Shem Tov and wondered: How could your spirit dance if you had lived through what Menachem Sassov had?

Daniel never asked, because he knew what the old man would say.

How could it not?

Daniel was thirty-six, a father seven times over, Menachem's right hand in all matters of business, a man whose calls those same developers and councilmen now answered personally, when the Admor brought him fully into the fold.

And still, Daniel hadn't been ready for what the Admor told him.

There was no future for their people in the only home they'd ever known, he said. The Sassovs were victims of their own success, their own fruitfulness. There was barely enough housing for them in Williamsburg, and tomorrow there would be more Sassovs and less space, and what space there was would be prohibitively expensive. The neighborhood was exploding with bars, restaurants, galleries, and office buildings, every one of them attracting more investment, luring more people.

It was time to begin the arduous, delicate, impossibly complex work of mass relocation, and so tomorrow Sassov Holdings LLC would tender an offer on a vast, undeveloped swath of land two hours north of Brooklyn, a wilderness that would someday be a city.

A homeland.

It was a solution wrapped in an existential crisis. The Sassovs lived in tension with the modern world—but they *lived in it*. Every practice and ritual was tailored to allow holiness to thrive here, in this specific place, this meticulously insulated community. These businesses and apartments had been in these families for generations, and the political capital that made it all possible had taken just as long to amass.

Uprooting the people was going to inflict a new version of an ancient trauma. This was unavoidable, Menachem explained, but it could be minimized. The Sassovs must not feel like refugees, forced to start over, or like settlers, coaxing sustenance from the soil of a strange land. The challenge before the two of them, Menachem and Daniel, was to figure out how to transfer all the Sassovs' power and influence—every alliance forged and favor done and favor owed, every partnership and arrangement—from Brooklyn to upstate.

Their success or failure would define the Admor's legacy and determine the Sassovs' future. Menachem believed it would take ten years.

Eight years later, the land still lay fallow—but the web of contracts, kickbacks, payoffs, investments, and shares of profit Daniel had built was a thing of beauty. He saw it in his mind as a literal web, rows and rows of silver threads arranged in perfect symmetry and balance, strong and inter-dependent and tenuous, any vibration along the outer vectors immediately detectable from his perch at the center.

In the end, the hard facts bore out what he had always known: the Sassovs could not build without destroying. Their exodus would create winners and losers, grant wealth and opportunity to some and snatch it violently from others.

But the thing about others was that they were others.

The city-to-come hinged on the teardown of three mas-sive housing projects in Brooklyn—each one currently thirty-three percent Sassov-occupied—and the construc-tion of the luxury high-rises that would replace them. This would completely transform Williamsburg, or perhaps com-plete the transformation of Williamsburg. And the Sassovs' thirty percent stake in both the demolition of the old build-ings and the construction, sale, and maintenance of the new ones would translate into billions of dollars—enough to build the new city, repaying old debts and incurring new ones through the bestowal of lucrative contracts along the way. It meant an overwhelming new voting bloc, enough to rewrite the political realities of their new congressional dis-trict and secure the Sassovs' autonomy in their new home.

The other sixty-seven percent of the projects' residents, well, they'd figure something out.

The proposal had to clear the City Council and the State Senate and Assembly, at which point the U.S. Depart-ment of Housing and Urban Development needed to sign off on it. The political fallout would be tremendous, so the profits and favors had to match.

And they did.

The fix was in, the votes were there—thanks in no small

part to the influence of the Vishnitzers and the Belzers, whose construction firms would consequently be handling demolition—and the new legislative session began in two weeks.

PX Construction, Nyack Hydro, Sebius Power, Langford Excavation, and Harriman Haul had been awarded the upstate contracts for the breaking of ground, the water and electrical infrastructure, the sewer system and sanitation services. A major component of each of their winning bids had been a quiet stroll across the rolling hills of the city-to-be with Daniel, as the companies' principals detailed their policies regarding direct investment, patronage jobs, and campaign contributions.

Where their answers lacked specificity, Daniel extended the web.

Closer to home, Councilman Shaka Robinson had sipped the Admor's tea and discussed his mayoral aspirations and the awful toll the housing projects' demise would take on those of his constituents who did not have a new homeland to which they could flee. Shaka had to oppose the bill, he told the Grand Rebbe. But in return for the citywide Hasidic vote, he would whip enough of his colleagues in the opposite direction to ensure that his principled stand did not derail the Admor's plans.

Evolve or die.

But if all his long years at the Admor's side had taught Daniel anything, it was that there was always one asshole who didn't want to play ball.

12

The Work of Creation

"So," Len said as he steered the van, "was your brother always such a dick?"

Up ahead, Pinchas flashed his cop lights and chirped his siren at a delivery truck trying to double-park. The driver sped off, probably thanking the God of his forebears that he had not been cited.

"No," said Miri. "Or if he was, I was too caught up in my own problems to notice. But I don't remember him being so angry." She gestured at Pinchas's SUV. "You have to be angry to do that job."

"If you're not angry, you're not paying attention," Len said, in that vague way he had. Was he talking about the Shomrim? People in general? Was he quoting something? If so, was it relevant, or was he just free-associating?

Pinchas turned the corner and pulled over in front of

the Grand Rebbe's palace, so wide it seemed to shoulder the buildings on either side out of its way. He parked behind another Shomrim SUV—both of them straddling the sidewalk for no reason Miri could discern except to prove that the laws of the goyish world didn't apply.

"So . . . now what?" asked Len, wheeling the van in behind him. "We just stroll Clay Thompson back there into the Grand Rebbe's living room?"

Miri took in the tableau through her shattered window; it had not changed since she'd been a kid, zagging three blocks out of her way just to walk past the Admor's house. A pair of Shomrim stood guard before the thigh-high wrought-iron gate at the foot of the stairs; a pair of gray-bearded rebbes descended the steps, deep in conversation, leather-bound tomes beneath their arms. A staid, ceremonious air hung heavy over the entire block, as befitted the domicile of a head of state. Miri looked over at Len, wondering if he could feel it.

"I'm sure someone will tell us," she said. And sure enough, a tall, strikingly handsome man was skimming down the steps with a grace and confidence Miri had seldom seen in a Hasid. It filled her with an unexpected rush of pride, or perhaps some heretofore undiscovered species of platonic lust.

Weird.

The Shomrim stood aside and the man opened the gate, beelined to Miri's window, and spoke to her in clipped, businesslike Yiddish.

"I'm Daniel Kempfer. I understand you have something to show me."

"I have something to show the Admor," she replied, speaking English for Len's benefit.

"Well," said Daniel, with a smile that did not so much disarm as shock her, "you might say I am the Admor's eyes and ears." His English was as good as hers—rare for a man, unless he worked an unusually goy-facing job.

"Where are his actual eyes and ears?" asked Miri.

Daniel smiled again, but the novelty was gone now. "May I please see?" he said, and Miri felt her will stiffen.

"I don't take orders from Sassov men anymore. There's a nine-foot golem in the back of this van who knew Menachem's grandfather, so you need to decide if you want to go get him, or if we should just leave. Either way is fine with us."

"No one is ordering you to do anything," said Daniel, and Miri started to doubt herself, felt an apology slide up her throat. Then Daniel snuck a look at Len—literally went over her head to lock eyes with the closest man he could find—and the apology slid back down and perished in a churning sea of stomach acid.

"I said what I said," Miri told him. It was a phrase she'd picked up at the bodega. She liked it because it sounded like something God would say.

Daniel turned and marched back the way he had come. He snapped something at the Shomrim, and they filed up the stairs behind him and vanished inside.

A few moments later they were back. One carried a large chair upholstered in red velvet. The other held what Miri at first thought was an umbrella. But as she watched the two of them unfold it in the passenger's side mirror, she realized it was actually a large sun tent, cathedral-ceilinged, closed on three sides and open on the fourth.

When it was set up behind the van, one of them lifted a walkie to his lips, and the palace doors opened, and out stepped Menachem Sassov.

The round black mink-trimmed hat set off the white curls of his hair, his beard. Miri had been bracing—hoping?—no, bracing to see the Admor enfeebled, skinny, leaning on a cane. But he was as sturdy as she remembered. He descended the stairs without even touching the handrail.

Miri walked around to the back of the van and slipped into the tent through the little breath of space the Shomrim had allowed. Len entered behind her, and they stared at the chair.

"I dare you to sit down," he said. Miri didn't bother to respond.

And then Menachem was there, five feet from her—and everything Miri had ever wanted to say to him was right inside her mouth, buzzing and bucking like the sins in the box Pandora opens in the Greek myth she'd read in the big illustrated children's book Adina had given her, Adina the second girl Miri had ever dated, who could not believe all that Miri did not know, Miri both grateful to learn and worried that she would not be able to tell if Adina misinformed her, that she would go around thinking some random thing was a canonical part of American culture when it was just garbage Adina happened to like or be nostalgic for. Those *Transformers* movies, for example. Those were clearly terrible.

Adonai our God hates hatred, she could say, had imagined saying. Or *This world you have built is no holier than any other,* or *Why don't you kiss the crack of my gay ass?* Or she could scandalize him, force sin upon him—grab his hand. That was all it would take. The touch of a woman who was not his wife. It was all so fragile.

But instead the Admor fixed his clear blue eyes on Miri and said, in Yiddish, "You are the youngest daughter of Gavrel and Feige Apfelbaum, is this not so?" and though she knew that this information had merely been whispered in his ear by Daniel, who stood close enough to whisper in it even now— that it did not mean he knew her or her people, who were no longer even hers—the words still left her speechless.

"If you want to come back to us, there are ways," the Grand Rebbe said, and Miri felt as though she couldn't breathe. Never in her wildest dreams on her single mattress in her rented room could she have imagined having this conversation.

But she also knew what the Grand Rebbe meant.

Marriage, children, a life of piety, the total annihilation of everything true.

"That's not why I'm here," she said, then turned away before the first tear came, and flung a hand in Len's direction.

He got it, nodded, and pulled up the door.

The Golem lay on his back, arms folded behind his head like he was stargazing. He sat up fast, as if embarrassed to be caught in a posture of such passivity.

"Here he is," said Miri, switching to English. "Grand Rebbe Menachem Sassov."

The Golem climbed out of the hold and stood before the Admor.

Menachem stepped back a pace, and craned his neck.

"Burekh ato adoynoy elohayni maylekh haoylem oyse mayse vereyshis," he whispered under his breath.

Blessed art thou, Lord our God, King of the Universe, who performs the work of creation.

Menachem backed up another pace—right into the chair, which Daniel had brought closer. The Admor plopped down on it, seemingly without noticing that it had not been there and now was. He continued to stare up at The Golem.

"I remember you," he said. "It took twenty of them to bind you. Six to shoot until your body crumbled into dust."

The Golem bent at the knee, supplicated himself before the Grand Rebbe.

"The Golem fail your grandfather," he said. "Get machine-gunned into pieces, like you say." He pointed at the letters etched into his forehead. "But Yehuda Sassov never rub off the aleph."

Miri wondered why The Golem was speaking English, until he turned and looked at Len. "Therefore, The Golem still belong to him. The Golem never get unmade, so cannot get made. And since Yehuda Sassov dead and you alive, The Golem serve you. Not this khokhem fun der hagode."

"Hold on a second," said Len. "What kind of rule is that? And what did you just call me?"

The Grand Rebbe stared at The Golem for a long time.

"Perhaps it is the will of Hashem that you be given another chance," he said at last, and for the most infinitesimal of moments, Miri thought the Admor was talking to her.

13

The Fuckboy Follies
of Geraldine Hardis-Burton

This was not, Len reflected, steering the van past endless, sprawling fields with shit growing in them, crops or whatever, as he followed Daniel and Menachem in the SUV just ahead, how he'd intended to spend his summer vacation.

But then, last summer had been pretty weird too.

Len was undoubtedly a top one percent earner among secondary-school art teachers in Brooklyn, especially if you factored in that he could eat lunch for free every day, and given the subpar nature of the restaurants in Brooklyn Heights—a handful of fuddy-duddy places that commanded the loyalty of the neighborhood's old rich people, plus an ever-proliferating variety of low-quality grab-and-go options for students and the hundreds of city workers who cut

through the park to Montague from the courts and adminis-
trative buildings every day—that was actually significant
value added. He had job security, insurance, a retirement
account.

But compared to his friends and neighbors, Len was still
broke. Waleed absolutely made more money than he did,
though it helped that Waleed didn't pay taxes. Waleed's girlfriend, Afruz, was a freelance graphic designer, and she made
more than either of them. Upstairs from Len, in the triplex,
lived a French hedge fund guy, Armond, with his wife and
two little kids; they'd been there for three years and paid ten
thousand a month and spent the summers in Avignon and
every weekend at their country place in Rhinebeck.

Len had been living in the garden apartment for ten
years, and his rent was fifteen hundred dollars. The owner,
an old lady in Florida who'd inherited the place from her
father, could have jacked him up to market rate at any
time, thirty-five hundo, maybe even four thousand, and
Len would have had to move. But she didn't seem to want
the hassle. Or maybe she was dead, and local kids had
been stealing his rent checks out of her mailbox and cash-
ing them at Western Union for the last five years—who
knew? If Len had a maintenance issue, he called Luis,
who lived on the block and had been a general contractor
in the Dominican Republic and could handle anything;
Luis charged Len and Len enclosed the invoice with his
rent check and deducted the amount, and Evelyn in Boca
never said a word.

Len had alchemized this confluence of absentee land-
lord, laissez-faire neighbors, low rent, and high demand

into a secondary income stream. Three years ago, he'd hired Afruz to take professional photographs of the apartment, and then listed it on Vrbo (formerly VRBO, Vacation Rentals By Owner, and pronounced V.R.B.O., then acquired, reacquired, rebranded, deacronymed, and currently pronounced "verbo," which struck Len as the name of a superhero in an elementary school grammar textbook) at three hundred dollars a night with a one-week minimum stay. When he got takers, he decamped to Waleed and Afruz's place in Carroll Gardens, slept on a blow-up mattress in their living room, and paid for dinner every night.

And just like that, Len was making an extra twenty grand a year and feeling like a brilliant young entrepreneur.

Then, last April, his buzzer had sounded and Len opened the door to find a beatific couple in their twenties standing on his threshold, suitcases in hand, their cab just pulling away from the curb.

"Uh, can I help you?" Len said.

The woman smiled. "Oui, Len, it is Elodie. And Julien. From France?"

"I'm sorry . . . do I know you?"

"We are your renters, for the gardener's apartment? We emailed? I wired you the money?"

Len shook his head. "I don't do that."

Elodie's smooth, tanned forehead scrunched up in befuddlement. "But . . . this is 21 Fillmore Place, yes? You are Len?"

"Yeah. But we didn't email. And whoever you wired money to, it wasn't me. How much did you wire?"

"Four thousand dollars," said Elodie.

She turned and spoke to Julien in French. He unzipped his backpack, took out his laptop, balanced it on his suitcase, and started to look for something.

Damn, thought Len, hating himself for it, I could have used four grand.

"Let me ask you this," he said. "Where did you see the rental listing?"

"On Craigslist," said Elodie.

Len shook his head. "I don't advertise on Craigslist."

Julien found what he was looking for and passed Elodie the laptop.

"This is the contract we signed."

Len peered at it. Not only was it a rental contract for his apartment, it was *his* rental contract. With his name typed out at the bottom, and an illegible signature that was not his illegible signature scrawled atop it.

"I'm very sorry," he said, feeling the panic start to simmer and the sweat bust out of his glands, "but this is not from me. Someone scammed you."

Elodie and Julien just looked at each other, and then Julien said, "Merde."

"Do you have the ad? The listing?"

"Oui." Julien pulled it up, and spun the laptop so Len could look.

It was his Vrbo listing. Someone had cloned it—and figured out his address, which did not appear in the ad. Len had no idea how you could do that, but what Len didn't know about the internet could fill a warehouse. Maybe it had been a former renter. Or— Fuck. He'd written "landmarked block" in the description, and Fillmore Place was the only landmarked block in Williamsburg. Henry Miller had lived there, then left when Jews from the Lower East Side started coming over the bridge.

Len had made it easy. Len had never thought to make it hard.

Elodie and Julien waited anxiously.

"So . . ." she said at last, "can we rent the apartment?"

"I'm sorry," said Len, and watched her face fall, "but it's not available. I've got renters coming tomorrow."

Julien threw up his hands.

"But what we are supposed to do?"

Len racked his brain. Was Armond home? he wondered loopily. Maybe he'd take in these fucked-over fellow Frenchies?

Armond one hundred percent would not.

"I honestly don't know," he said. "I'm so sorry this happened. And I'm going to get to the bottom of it."

Elodie looked like she might cry. "Okay, well . . . goodbye," she said.

Julien was not ready to go. He pointed a finger at Len. "How do we know it is not you who scam us?"

Len said the first thing that came to mind. "Because I wouldn't do that." He thought some more. "Why would I be here, if I'd scammed you and I knew you were coming?"

"To scam us some more," said Julien, but he didn't sound sure.

Len took out his phone. "Look, I'm about to call the police, because this is just as much of a problem for me as it is for you. We can all talk to them together if you want."

Elodie shook her head. "There is no point," she said. "Come on, Julien. We must find a place to sleep."

He picked up his suitcase.

"I'm sorry for your trouble," Elodie said as she walked through the gate, and Len couldn't discern any sarcasm, but she was French. He felt like an asshole, but he was a victim here. What was he supposed to do, let them crash on his couch? For all he knew they were scamming him.

Except, no, they weren't.

He watched them turn the corner, then went back inside and called Vrbo. A very pleasant twenty-year-old who'd clearly never been the victim of fraud or even light bullying told him he had to contact law enforcement in the jurisdiction where the money was sent.

Len went on Craigslist, and sure enough, there was the listing. His text, his photos. They'd lowered his prices a little, so the place was even more enticing.

Len responded, pretending to be a renter from Australia coming to town for her son's graduation from NYU. He spent three hours drafting the email—building his character, researching Australian terms and spellings, deciding what questions to ask. It was the best, most satisfying writing he'd done in years.

An hour later, Len got a response, with wiring information. The bank was in Dover, Delaware. He picked up his phone, called the Dover police department, and explained his situation to the desk sergeant.

A detective would call him right back.

A detective did not.

Len waited an hour and called again. The line went straight to voicemail.

Len called Waleed, because he needed to get high.

Waleed reminded him that he was supposed to come

over that night anyway—he had renters booked. So Len went to Waleed and Afruz's place, and prospective renter Geraldine Hardis-Burton of Melbourne, Australia, wrote another email. Was the neighborhood safe to walk in at night? Was there a supermarket nearby?

Then Len and Waleed got super high.

The scammer wrote back and said the closest supermarket was three blocks away, and the neighborhood was safe—both true. His name, Rick Jones, was generically American, but his English was imperfect. A clue.

For the next three days, as Waleed and Afruz went about their business, Len pursued vigilante justice from the couch.

"So then I tell him I went to wire the money," he told Waleed, on a walk around the neighborhood that Waleed had insisted they take, "but my bank said his account number was too long. And without missing a beat, he's like 'No problem, here's another one.' This one's in Galveston, Texas. The one after that's in California—I keep making up excuses and he keeps handing them out. So I'm calling the cops in all these different places to see if they can help, but nobody can. Some cop in Nevada told me to submit a claim to the FBI's fraud division. So I did that. But I'm getting nowhere. I can't even get a call back. And meanwhile, this guy is pressuring me to book the apartment."

"This doesn't seem like a good use of your time," Waleed said.

"Bro, my renters called me today. Some Brazilian guy showed up at my door, saying he'd rented the place, he wired money—the same thing all over again. He scared the shit out of them, too. I ended up giving them a free night. If I get one bad Vrbo review, I'm fucked."

"Can't you just get Craigslist to take down the ad?"

"They already took it down three times. These mother-fuckers just repost it. It's a big game of Whac-A-Mole. So finally I write to Rick Jones and I'm like, listen, can I pay you with a credit card? Other rental sites take credit cards. And the dude is like, 'I used to do that, but clients tried to de-fraud me, so I stopped.'"

"Ballsy," said Waleed.

"So then I'm like, look, my son-in-law is in New York, can you just call him and talk this out, and he can bring you a check? And he says sure. So I get a burner phone, and I'm all ready to play the son-in-law, who's this Lebanese stock trader named Samer—"

"What? Why?"

"I don't know, why the fuck not?"

"Why would you pretend to be Lebanese, when I'm *actually* Lebanese?"

"I mean, I didn't want to pull you any further into this bullshit. But anyway, dude never calls. I think he's running out of patience. But I've got a new plan. I'm gonna decrypt his IP address."

"You don't know how to do that."

"Nah, but I found a girl on Bumble who's in cybersecu-rity, so I asked her on a date."

Waleed considered this.

"It's good to see you motivated, at least," he said.

Len's date, though not successful by conventional mea-sures, yielded an IP address.

"I'm going to Stockholm," he told Waleed that night, al-ready shopping for a ticket. "Wanna come?"

"I've got a cousin in Norway," Waleed said.

"I don't see how that's relevant."

"You buying my ticket?"

"Fuck it. Sure."

"And we're gonna do what, exactly?"

"Settle up."

"Walk me through this," said Waleed. "Pretend I have no idea how we're going to settle up with some international cartel of Swedish Craigslist scam artists."

"We land, we go to a hardware store, we buy a pole saw and a pickax, and we go knock on the door like 'What's up, motherfucker? I live at 21 Fillmore Place in Brooklyn. Sound familiar?'"

"And then . . . we murder everybody with a pole saw and a pickax?"

"We come to an understanding."

"What does that mean, an understanding?"

Len sighed and looked out over the treetops lining Waleed's block. "Well, one scenario is that when they see that I'm a real person—that they've caused real harm to a real person, not just an address they found on the internet—they realize that they have to make it right."

"Like reimburse you or something?"

"Maybe. Yeah. I don't know."

"I mean . . . it's a beautiful vision of human nature. What's the other scenario?"

"In the other scenario, I also show them I'm a real person. But with the pole saw."

Waleed seemed ready to object, so Len rushed on.

"Listen, don't worry. It's probably just some putz living in his mom's basement. I Google-Earthed the address. It's way out in the sticks. And it's Sweden, dude. They don't even have guns. If you kill somebody, you get like ten years in jail."

"It disturbs me that you know that," said Waleed. "Forget it. I'll stay home."

"I'm just saying, it's a nonviolent place, with progressive ideas about incarceration. Their prisons are actually fucking beautiful. If those cells were in Brooklyn, they'd rent for more than my apartment."

"You seem excited about going to a Swedish prison."

"I'm not. I promise. I just went down a rabbit hole. Now am I booking you a ticket, or what?"

Twenty-six hours later, Len and Waleed were sitting on a bus en route from Gamla Stan, in central Stockholm, to Nacka, a rural suburb to the city's west. Len held a pole saw, Waleed a pickax.

The bus let them off at the top of a sloping street lined with trees, the glossy surface of a lake visible here and there between the canopies. They followed it down to the bottom, where a mailbox confirmed that this was the house they sought. It sat right on the lake, which was bigger than it looked from higher up, the perimeter studded with small docks to which modest boats were moored. Evening sunlight played on the water. It was seven-thirty and it wouldn't get dark until eleven, which didn't help with the jet lag.

"This is dope," said Waleed. "I would live here."

"Let's do this," said Len. He marched up to the house and thwacked the big brass knocker against the door three times.

The woman who opened it was tall, with green eyes, most of her long black hair pulled back in a slightly off-center ponytail, with a single loose strand curling down over her left cheek, almost to her full top lip. She was wearing an apron over a T-shirt and a long summery skirt, and holding a butcher's knife that had some strands of translucent white flesh stuck to it—bits of raw cod, it looked like. Len didn't register any of these details, would have flunked a pop quiz on the particulars. He knew only that she had one of the most stunning faces he'd ever seen this close, and definitely the most stunning he'd ever seen while holding a pole saw.

She looked unfazed by the haggard stranger at her door, or the second haggard stranger in her driveway. It did not seem to have occurred to her that she might be in danger— it was certainly not the reason she was holding the knife. There was a calm to Sweden that Len and Waleed had noticed right away, and attributed to the social safety net. Nobody here was worried that if they broke a leg or their car got towed, they'd end up on the street.

Len decided immediately that she lived alone; people had a certain energy about them, in their homes, when they did. He knew it in himself, and he recognized it in others. Or perhaps he just wanted this woman to be the reason he'd come here. He'd never wanted to settle up with someone so badly.

"Kan jag hjälpa dig?" she asked, and when she saw that he didn't understand, she switched to English.

"Can I help you?" Her accent wasn't Swedish; it might have been Arabic. There was extra length to the *a*, something eel-like to the *l*.

It occurred to Len that he had failed to think this through, and that whatever he'd been planning to do, he was not planning to do anymore. Perhaps he only believed that violence could be justice in the abstract—or perhaps he only believed in himself in the abstract, and had been propelled here not by his own will but the satisfaction, the momentum, he'd found in creating a character.

He summoned up a garbled, ridiculous accent he could not hope to speak in with any consistency, a mixture of every impression he'd ever attempted: shades of Pepe Le Pew and Inigo Montoya, a little Foghorn Leghorn, some Crocodile Dundee. But whatever it was, it wasn't American.

"Hello," he said. "We're your renters. I'm Rodigan. From Guyana." Len knew nothing about Guyana, except that it was the only English-speaking country in South America. "By way of New Zealand," he added, to muddy the waters. "Pleased to make your acquaintance."

Waleed was beside him now, backing the play. "And this is me mate—"

"Fela," said Waleed. "From Nigeria." He made no attempt at an accent.

The woman shook her head. "You have the wrong house," she said, and started to close the door.

"No, no, no!" said Len. "We emailed! I wired you four thousand dollars! This is the house in the ad! Tranquil lakeside retreat in Nacka, twenty minutes from the South End!" He pointed inside. "I even recognize your hallway!"

She paused, taking that in. "Where did you see this ad?"

"On Airbnb." He tried his best to look stricken, and turned his stricken face to Waleed so that he too might stricken himself. "Please, what are you telling me, Miss?"

She sighed, and rubbed at her eyes. "This is a very common scam."

"Scam?" Waleed repeated, practically clutching his pearls. "Scam?"

Down a notch, thought Len. You're Nigerian.

She beckoned with her knife. "Come in. I will explain."

Len followed her down the hallway and into a bright kitchen with lake views and a tulip table. He couldn't help but think about Elodie and Julien. He hadn't let them inside his house. He hadn't done shit for them. This woman was not just luminous, but kind.

He was going to forgive her, and it was going to be amazing. It was going to be tikkun olam. He just had to figure out how to get there.

"Would you like some tea?" she asked when Len and Waleed were seated, their bags and weapons piled on the floor, her knife resting on a blond wood cutting board, the soup she had been making abandoned.

Her kettle was sleek, bright red, electric. This whole place was just so incredibly fucking Scandinavian. She sat down in the last empty chair.

"I am Hadil," she said, pressing a hand to her breastbone. "What they do is find an old listing and copy everything. Then they make a fake one on a different site, and trick people into sending them money."

"Who would do such a thing?" said Len, really feeling into his aghastness, his disappointment at man's inhumanity to man. "Taking advantage of a traveler—that's the lowest of the low."

"In my country," said Waleed, "you would be put to death."

Hadil glanced at their tools.

"What brings you to Stockholm?" she asked.

Len had an answer at the ready.

"The international carpentry competition. We met in trade school, in Switzerland. Decided to team up. But that was when we had a place to stay." He shook his head. "I saved for months to afford this trip."

"Me too," Waleed said. "And I need the prize money for little Zinka's operation."

Len shot him a *too much* look, but Hadil didn't seem to have registered the comment. She stood and awakened her laptop, open to a cooking website.

"There is a youth hostel nearby. I think it is very cheap."

She typed in a search term, then picked up her cell, dialed, and spoke in Swedish.

The kettle clicked off just as the call ended, steam billowing into the air. "They have no vacancies," Hadil reported.

Len dropped his head into his hands and evinced great consternation.

"So who has our money?" he asked after a while.

"You'll never know," Hadil answered. "They could be anywhere." She poured the tea, then took a round tin of butter cookies out of a cabinet and placed them on the table.

"I am Iraqi," she said. "I came here seven years ago. Sweden allowed me to immigrate. They gave me Swedish classes, for free. I took three years' worth, until my Swedish sounded just like theirs. I have a degree in civil engineering, but if your name is Hadil Nuriddin, they will not give you a decent job. All the Iraqis live in one part of town, signs all in Arabic, Iraqi restaurants, Iraqi hookah bars. Half of them are on public assistance. The Swedes write articles about it in their newspapers, trying to understand. Asking why we don't assimilate into society."

Len sipped his tea. Was it possible he had forgiven her already? That he could forgive her without ever revealing himself, based purely on her kindness to the person he was pretending to be?

It seemed a little much.

"Is this the Iraqi neighborhood?" Waleed asked.

Hadil smiled and shook her head. "No, it is not."

"So what do you do, Hadil?" said Len.

"I scam tourists on Craigslist," Hadil said. "So that I can live on this lake. But I am not a bad person, Len Bronstein from Brooklyn."

Len stood up so fast he banged his thighs against the tulip table and knocked it over.

Hadil's tea spilled into her lap, and she screamed. The other two mugs smashed against the floor.

"How do you know who I am?" he demanded.

"It was a guess," said Hadil, wringing out her skirt. "I knew you were not from Guyana and Nigeria. And then I thought about all those emails, from the Australian lady, what's her name."

"Geraldine Hardis-Burton," said Len with pride and affection, as if she were his grandmother.

"Yes. She was not believable."

"Oh, fuck you she wasn't," said Len. "She was great." He stared at the pole saw, considered snatching it up. But for what?

It was time to admit the pole saw has been a waste of money.

"So now what?" asked Hadil.

"You tell me," Len shot back. Waleed got down on his knees and started picking up mug shards.

"You're the one who—what, decrypted my IP address and came out here with whatever that is," she said, pointing at the pole saw. "Is that what you did, by the way?"

"Yeah."

Hadil stood. "I've got to fire my IT guy."

Len pointed a finger, halving the space between them.

"Stop sending people to my house."

"Fine."

"Reimburse me for my flight, and Waleed's flight, and the pickax and the pole saw."

"Waleed is Fela?"

"Ahlan," Waleed said. "Kaif halek?"

"Bkheir wa enta," said Hadil, then turned back to Len. "Did it ever occur to you to just email me and say, like, *I'm the real owner of this apartment, stop fucking about with it*?"

"No," said Len. "Why, what would you have done?"

"I would have stopped fucking about with it. I've got hundreds of listings, man. Most of which rent for more than yours. And sorry, but I'm not paying for your flights. Not when you didn't even try emailing me first."

"Why didn't you email her first?" Waleed asked.

"Because it would have blown my cover." Len paced the kitchen, rubbing the back of his neck. "We have no place to stay," he said. "Let us stay here."

Hadil shrugged. "Fine. Just don't break anything else."

"Do you have a boat?" asked Waleed.

The Big Rip-Off

"This is never going to work," said Miri, as the Rebbe's SUV pulled over in front of them—though *pulled over* was wrong. It simply stopped, because the dirt road did.

And if she was understanding things correctly—and maybe she wasn't, because as soon as they got what they wanted from her, Daniel and the Admor had stopped taking questions and started giving orders—the end of the road was where the Sassovs intended to begin the road.

"There's a joke," she told Len, "about a Jewish man who gets shipwrecked on a desert island. After twenty years he gets rescued, and the rescuers are amazed to see that he's made a bunch of buildings out of driftwood, and they ask for a tour. So he says *Here is the synagogue, which was of course the first thing I built. Here is my house. Here is my store, where*

I sell myself coconuts. Here is another synagogue. They're like, *Wait, why would you build two synagogues?* And he says—"

"'*This* one I pray in, and *this* one I wouldn't be caught dead in!'" finished Len. "Come on. I may not speak Yiddish, but I know *that* one."

Miri gazed out at the empty land. "That's the problem with this place," she said. "There won't be any second synagogue."

Len checked the time on his phone. "Hard to believe we're only two hours from Williamsburg," he said. "Shitty cell service, though."

"They'll build towers."

"*They* won't, but somebody will. And that sly old fucker will make money off it. They've got all the angles figured out."

Miri bristled. She might hate the Admor, but he was the Admor, and it wasn't right to talk about him as if he were just some businessman.

Daniel, on the other hand.

"I hate everything about this," Len said, cutting the engine. "I'm not some fuckin' golem chauffeur. If he's gonna pledge allegiance to the king of the Jews, the king of the Jews can rent his own van."

"I'm not letting them take him away from us," said Miri. "At least this keeps us . . ."

She trailed off, and Len finished her sentence.

"What, *in the game?* Let me tell you what I've learned about playing games I don't understand, Miri: I'm not smart enough or ruthless enough to win them. And these guys have an army. Literally an army. I should let The Golem out right now, turn around, and go home. He can wander the forests until he finds a nice lady bigfoot who's down to raise the kids Jewish."

A pickup truck was rambling up behind them, stirring the dust. Len stopped blathering to watch it in the mirror, and Miri did the same.

The man who climbed out was sixtyish, wore boots and jeans, a John Deere hat. At first, Miri assumed he was just some local who'd spotted them from the main road, half a mile back, and taken a few minutes out of his day to make sure they weren't lost, since this was about the last place in the world anybody would deliberately drive a moving van.

Daniel tapped on Len's window, and he and Miri jumped. "That's him," he said. "Let's go."

Len rolled down the window. "Everybody?"

"Just you two. Stand behind the van and keep your mouths shut."

"Then why—"

"Because you'll be less suspicious than you would be sitting here."

Menachem was shaking the man's hand when they emerged. He was a foot taller than the Admor, all lank and limbs except for the potbelly spilling over his big belt buckle, and he moved with a kind of lanky, gestural rhythm, like a man who wanted to convey the idea that he embodied the natural grace of the land.

"Hello, Mr. Kempfer," he said, turning and nodding at Daniel.

"Hello, Congressman," said Daniel. A curt nod at Miri and Len. "These are some associates of ours." Then right back to the congressman, who no more matched Miri's mental image of a congressman than this featureless vista matched her idea of a Hasidic enclave or she, in her pilly cardigan, loose hair, and jeans probably matched his notion of a Sassov associate.

"Pleasure," he said, without bothering to look at them. "So." He spread his arms. "Here I am. This better be good."

"It could be very good, Carl. It's been good for Russo. For Hollis. For Garrity. For Baumeister."

Carl smiled without opening his lips. "But it's still my committee, Mr. Kempfer. And they can't raise their hands if I don't bring it to a vote, now can they?"

"No, they cannot," said Daniel. "So tell me what that's going to take, and we'll make it happen. "

The congressman hooked both his thumbs over his belt buckle and rocked forward and back on the stacked heels of his boots. "What it's gonna take," he repeated, and looked up at the wide blue sky as if he were thinking about it. But even Miri could tell that he was not.

"How about I go buy a nice acorn-fed pig down at the Johnson Farm," he said, looking back down at Daniel, "and I slow-cook the whole thing up and have my housekeeper Rosa make her famous carnitas, and we give the Rabbi a knife and fork. And when he eats every last delicious morsel, that's when I'll move your land use bill and your water bill and your sanitation bill and all your other goddamn bills through my committee."

Menachem sighed the sigh of a man disappointed in one of his children—disappointed, but not surprised.

Daniel folded his hands in front of him and said nothing. A moment passed, and then another.

It was funny, thought Miri, how quickly a threat or a provocation or whatever this was started losing power in the face of silence. The person who'd issued it had to ramp it up even further, which made whatever they'd said already seem insufficient, or they had to stand and wait, which was a form of supplication.

Daniel stroked his beard and stared out at the Sassov land.

"Why is it that everyone but you can see how good this will be for your district?" he said at last. "An investment of billions, Congressman Mazeroski. Who says no to that?"

"I say no to that," Mazeroski snapped. "Because if I say yes, it won't be my district anymore. You'll overrun it. Like—"

He broke off.

He wanted to say rats, thought Miri. Leeches. Parasites. Vampires. Cancer.

"You are up for reelection in a year," Menachem Sassov said mildly.

"You wanna *primary* me?" sneered Mazeroski. "Be my guest." He turned toward an imaginary audience and gripped an invisible mic. "Friends, my opponent here is the carpet-bagging puppet of a powerful, secretive, ultrareligious Jewish sect that wants to take over the community you call home and turn it into . . . who knows what? Israel? Some fur-hat-wearing Russian ghetto from three hundred years ago? We all know how this goes. They'll pour in by the tens of thousands, all dressed exactly alike—because they don't think for themselves, they just do whatever their leader says. Next, they'll overwhelm the voter rolls. Take over the school board. Worm their way into everything. Reelect Carl Mazeroski, or you'll spend the rest of your life under the thumb of the fuckin' Jews!" He pointed his long arm at the Admor. "Whaddaya think, Rabbi, you think that plays?"

"It probably does," said Daniel. "Antisemitism is still with us, unfortunately."

"Here we go," said Mazeroski, rolling his eyes. "It's not antisemitism if it's the goddamn truth."

"I'd like to show you something that may cause you to reconsider your position," said Daniel. He shooed away Miri and Len and opened up the van.

Mazeroski peered into the gloom.

"What the hell have you got in there?" he asked.

Out vaulted The Golem, landing so hard that the dry, packed earth beneath his feet cracked like ice on a lake.

"It is a golem," said Menachem. "Praise Hashem."

"Rip off his arms," said Daniel.

The Golem grunted an assent and started toward Mazeroski.

The Admor pushed back the brim of his hat and dabbed his forehead with a folded handkerchief. "We must safeguard our future, Congressman," he said. "For far too long, our fate has been in the hands of men like you."

Mazeroski appeared to be having difficulty breathing. He dropped to his knees before The Golem, clutching at his chest. He looked from one face to the next, his eyes pleading for help. When they landed on Miri, she felt as if she'd been electrocuted.

The Golem bent, knocked off Mazeroski's hat, and sniffed his head. "Smell like Jew-hater," he said, and grabbed both the congressman's wrists.

"Hold on," said Daniel. "Wait." The Golem dropped Mazeroski's arms, and the man fell over onto his side.

"Are you perhaps willing to rethink your position?" Daniel asked the unconscious congressman.

"Stop!" Miri shouted. "What's wrong with you?" She dodged past The Golem and knelt beside Mazeroski. He didn't seem to be breathing. Miri twisted to look at Len. "Do something!" she screamed, not because she thought he could but because he was the only other person present who might try.

"I think it's cardiac arrest," said Len, coming over and crouching next to her. He stared up at The Golem. "You scared him to death."

The Golem turned to Daniel. "So not rip off arms?"

Miri stood and felt the blood rush to her head. "This is all bullshit," she said, and pushed The Golem as hard as she could. He didn't budge, but she had his full attention.

"Is this what you want to do?" she demanded. "Intimidate politicians? You think that helps the Jews?" She pointed at Menachem. "You think it's what his grandfather would have wanted?"

"The Golem don't think," The Golem said. "The Golem do what The Golem told."

"Get back in the van," said Daniel. "All of you. We're done here."

"Wait a minute," said Miri to The Golem. "Hold on. Look at this." She reached into her pocket, took out her phone, pulled up a video she'd saved, and thrust it in his face.

It was from Charlottesville, Virginia. Hundreds of white men in polo shirts filled the frame, their faces contorted, hatred oozing from their pores. Each one held a torch, and they chanted as they marched.

Jews will not replace us! Jews will not replace us!

The Golem stared at them, transfixed.

"You asked who wants to kill us," said Miri. "Here they are."

The Golem furrowed his tremendous brow and clenched his giant fists. "Where?"

"Not here," Miri said.

"Kentucky," said Len. "This Tuesday." He winced as if speaking against his will, or his better judgment. "There was an article in the *Times* about it. A SMALL TOWN BRACES FOR A FAR RIGHT STORM."

"Okay," Miri implored The Golem. "That's where. That's when. Let's go."

The Golem spun and looked at Daniel, Menachem. He was desperate for their approval, Miri could tell.

"No," the Grand Rebbe said. "That is not our fight. That is not our world."

The Golem was quiet.

"World is world," he said at last.

"World is world," repeated Miri. She took The Golem's arm and started to lead him toward the van.

Halfway there, he shook her off. "The Golem sick of traveling in dark," he said, and pointed at the Admor's SUV. "Open."

Daniel shook his head. "You belong to the Admor. You said so."

"The Golem never use the word 'belong,'" said The Golem.

Len stepped in front of Daniel and did the last thing in the world Miri expected: he quoted Hillel the Elder.

"If I am not for myself, who will be for me?" he asked, reaching into Daniel's suit pocket and extracting his key fob.

Daniel caught his wrist, and The Golem stepped forward and made a low sound deep in his throat.

Daniel let go.

Len pressed a button, and the trunk of the SUV yawed open.

The Golem leaned inside, and with a great rending of metal and leather, he ripped out the last row of seats and flung it behind him.

"Here," said Len, dropping the van key into Daniel's pocket. "You can return it to the U-Haul place on Atlantic. You know where that is, right?"

The Golem grunted and tore the middle row of seats out of the SUV. He carried it over to the van and tossed it inside, then hefted the back row and shoved that in as well.

The Admor clasped his hands together, opened his mouth, and said nothing.

He was bad at this, Miri realized. When was the last time anyone had refused to recognize his authority?

Well, anyone Jewish, Miri amended, looking over at Mazeroski, already coated in a fine layer of dust.

Well, anyone he would consider Jewish, she amended again, thinking of herself.

"You cannot go," the Grand Rebbe said finally, in Yiddish. "Hashem has made you what you are, and you must hold fast to that."

"I couldn't have put it better myself," Miri said, and got into the car.

The Golem crawled into his newly remodeled quarters and pulled the trunk lid down behind him. Len put the SUV in drive and made a wide, slow U-turn, around Daniel and the Admor and the body and the van and the pickup.

He rolled down his window and shot them a peace sign. The first time a customer had used the gesture to bid her goodbye, Miri had thought it was a V, for vagina—that this random Albanian construction worker was acknowledging and celebrating her lesbianism. Lucky, she had looked it up on the internet as soon as he left.

"Two Jews, three opinions," Len said by way of farewell, and before Miri could ask him what possible relevance that had here, the Sassovs lay behind them and the open road stretched out ahead.

Search Hymietown

"**W**hy'd you smell that asshole?" Len asked, once they were on the freeway.

"The Golem not smell asshole, The Golem smell head."

"Why'd you smell that asshole's head?"

"Find out if he hate Jews."

Len glanced over at Miri to see if this made any more sense to her than it did to him, then lifted slightly off the seat so he could use the rearview mirror to look The Golem in the eye. Even with all the seats removed, he seemed to fill the whole space. It was a good thing the Admor's car had tinted windows, or they'd have been famous already.

"You're telling me you can smell antisemitism?"

The Golem bounced a withering look off the mirror.

"Why haven't you mentioned this before?"

"The Golem not smell it before. Only goy The Golem meet Waleed, and Waleed cool."

"Any other amazing powers you've neglected to mention?"

The Golem shrugged, and his shoulders rippled like a landslide. "Could crush your head like walnut. That count?"

He poked the back of Miri's seat with his index finger. "Play video again."

"You've seen it enough," said Miri without turning around.

He poked harder.

"Fine," said Miri. She twisted, tapped.

"Jews will not replace us!" the marchers shouted, for the umpteenth fucking time. "Jews will not replace us!"

The clip was only forty-five seconds. Miri had tried to show The Golem some other footage—there was no shortage of neo-Nazis, Proud Boys, white nationalists, replacement theorists, and other assorted fuckbags to be found on YouTube, and Len got the sense that Miri had done more than a little spelunking of those rancid depths. But The Golem was singularly fixated on this video.

He watched it three more times, then said, "They think we are white?"

"No, they think we are *not* white."

"They are right. We are Jewish." The Golem thought for a moment. "If they know we not white, why they afraid we replace them?"

"It's complicated," said Len, then added, "these days."

They flew by a sign advertising the fast food options available at the upcoming exit. By rote, Len ranked them one through four, then wondered when the last time was that he'd actually eaten.

"The Jews—Ashkenazi Jews, Eastern European Jews, everybody in this car—we're kind of white now, in this country," he explained, already feeling unequal to the task. "We pass as—we're seen as white. Except by racists. They think that Jews have some kind of secret, hive-minded conspiracy and we're all working together to destroy the white race and the whole power structure that keeps white Christians on top. And that we're doing it by pretending to be white. So they're calling us out on that. But also, they think that as the secret puppet-masters of the world, we want to replace them in the workforce with immigrants. Or Black people. Or, I dunno, robots. So it's got a couple meanings."

The Golem thought about that for a while.

"From what The Golem remember," he said slowly, "for most of history, everybody hate Jews because Jews not want . . . how you say? Tsupasn zikh."

"Assimilate," said Miri.

"Well yeah, there's that too. Being white is a pretty new option for us. Nobody, almost nobody, was always white in America. Not the Irish, not the Italians, not the Poles. It's kind of like the mafia. Every once in a while, whiteness opens the books and admits new members, so white people have the numbers to keep running shit. But if you say yes, you gotta play by their rules. So like, when they opened the books for us, we walked away from the civil rights movement. And told ourselves we were doing it because Black people had walked away from us."

Len felt a surge of pride at how well he was explaining this, then realized that these were not his ideas. He was paraphrasing a poem he'd read last year as part of a mandatory four-day teacher training on racial sensitivity.

"Miri," he said, "do me a favor. Google 'Committed to Memory,' by . . . fuck. Some poet. It explains this really well." He snapped his fingers. "Brodsky."

Miri typed it in. The girl knew her way around the internet, that was for sure. "This is really long," she said, scrolling through.

"Try to find the part about the 'book of whiteness,' or something like that. Or, no, search 'Hymietown.'"

Miri searched, found, and started reading.

16

Brodsky (Excerpted)

in the liberal northeast
the prevailing attitude
regarding race descended
from that of the puritan
forebears toward sex:
neither touch nor speak of
those vexed & pernicious
things down there, lest
you sully the delicate
myth of your innocence
forever. it was the doctrine
of color-blindness: you
mentioned the hue of
a man's shirt when you
described him but not

the tone of his skin.
somehow this coquettish
lie became a badge of
virtue. it went without
saying that the color you
swallowed back down
your esophagus was only
ever black, because you
would not think to call
another white man,
white woman, white
child white. the virtue
was in pretending
not to notice blackness,
according it the same
invisibility, the same
casual irrelevance you
in your skin enjoyed.
but it is only by saying
black that white people
in america have spoken
themselves into existence.
& when whiteness recruits,
makes new made men,
flops open the thick
registry & dips the quill
into the inkwell, that
too is an erasure,
a devil's bargain,
a handshake conducted
while leaning over an abyss.

it is said that things
do not outpace their
naming, the prison
house of language &
all that shit. but children
can squeeze their heads
through the bars, are flush
with knowledge not yet
tethered to words. long
before they learn to count,
they want things to be fair.
the need might surface as
a love of symmetry,
a parceling of objects, a
rigorous accounting of
to whom what belongs.
it is selfish, at first, but
not finally—not always.
a child who rails against
the inequitable allocation
of cookies is closer to
putting her life on
the line for justice
than almost anyone
knows. the nameless
thing i tasted on the
air like salt was made
of shame, distance,
hypocrisy, silence—each
the engine of the next,

a perpetual motion machine
that hummed unnoticed
like an air conditioner &
like an air conditioner it
altered every breath.
something was wrong,
rotten. there was not
a single moment i
awakened to this, no
catalyzing incident, no
embryonic divergence
from the growth pattern
of my genotype. the
blade slips when you
try to cut; aphrodite
smothers the battlefield
with fog, shields paris
from his reckoning so
he can scuttle off to
fight another day.
there i was, a tiny knife
inside my tiny hand,
turning circles in the
dust, sure everyone
was lying, abstractly
furious & concretely
alone, listening as
hard as i could for the
whispered name of
the conspiracy that

bound the world—
which suggests i
suspected that it
implicated me, might
be spoken in my ear
shot.

there are margins,
shoulders, places that
bracket & outskirt
communities. we march
toward them or get
shunted there & live
circumscribed by their
dimensions. jewishness
is brackets upon brackets
upon brackets—think of
that when next you see
that echo, that ((( ))) mandibled
around our names with vile
intent & then repurposed.
judaism is the hotel
california of religions.
no matter how alienated
or ambiguous you feel
you cannot go anywhere
except the margins of
the margins, an escape
raft bigger than the ship.
there is a joke about a

jew who converts, enrolls
in seminary, studies for
years, becomes a priest,
gets his own congregation.
the night before he is meant
to give his first sermon
he cannot sleep, writes
& rewrites fitfully until
at last the fateful moment
comes. he takes the podium,
gazes out into the crowd &
takes a deep breath &
says *good morning, my
fellow goyim.*

there is the
otherness of being
a jew & the otherness
of not being jewish
enough. there is
the venerable civil
rights alliance, though
i watched it collapse
in grade school, when
the musty ledger fell
open & the disembodied
hand that gripped the
dripping quill materialized
to hover above the page.
the jews were finally

a few sinister gestures
away, had only to power
through hell week &
the fraternity would
throw open its iron-
plumped arms. &
wouldn't you know it,
right on cue here's jesse
jackson, poised to win
the democratic nomination
until he calls new york
city hymietown, & what
does whiteness ask of us?
only that we imbue the
reverend's word with
blood venom, erase
the history of the man
who said it until he is
nothing else, has never
stood on a motel balcony
in his life, & at the same
time claim he speaks
for all of black america
when he says hymietown—

hymietown! it sounds like
quaint ad copy from the
new york board of tourism,
*this summer, why not stop on
by & visit hymietown! we've*

got the best bagels & lox
you've ever tasted, & that's
a promise! or for a real
treat, take in a show at the
yiddish theater, then swing
by katz's for an egg cream!
hymietown! you & your
family will want to keep
on comin' back for years
to come!

—& make ourselves
believe that he means
us real harm, has unlidded
the simmering cauldron of
our former bedfellows'
secret treachery & must
be banished to a realm
of infamy from whence
there can be no escape,
from whence decades
later your right of
return is still denied. do
not confuse it with the
time-out corner to which
you will be lovingly
escorted for declaring
that *jews are responsible*
for all the wars in the
history of the world if

you are noted white
historian mel gibson, to
sober up for eighteen
minutes before the anti-
defamation league invites
you over to nosh on some
latkes & have a nice
productive chat.

Bunch of Whiny Losers

"If you think clay monster who just learn English yesterday understand all that, you giant dickhead," said The Golem.

"But you understood some of it," said Len, hoping this was true.

"Couple thing," The Golem said begrudgingly. "Joke about Jew who become priest pretty good. The Golem know actual Jew who become priest once."

"Wow," said Len. "There's gotta be a story there!"

"It short story. They decide he still Jew and aroysgerisn di kishkes durkhn tokhes."

"Ripped his guts out through his ass," Miri explained.

"Unpleasant," said Len.

"That Spanish Inquisition in nutshell."

"Also," said Len, emboldened toward chumminess by

the road-trip vibe the three of them had going here and even, to his chagrin, the almost-friendly way The Golem had just called him a giant dickhead, "can I just say? Enough with the whole *The Golem so dumb, The Golem can't think* routine already, dude. You learned English in one day. You're fucking smart. You could probably even learn to stop referring to yourself in the third person, if you wanted."

"The Golem never say . . ." The Golem paused and started over. "*I* never say *I* dumb." He grimaced, shook his head. "Sound wrong." He stared out the window for a while: shrub brush and median strip, forest beyond, a whole lot of nothing as far as Len was concerned.

"What The Golem say is not *can't* think. *Don't* think. Because The Golem always serve, so always have purpose." He poked Miri's seat, then Len's. "But *you,* and *you*— You fucking millennials."

Len laughed. "How do you know about millennials?"

"From Larry David. Also, this not The Golem first millennium."

"So what, you're saying that people born between twenty BCE and one AD were . . ."

The Golem nodded. "Bunch of whiny losers."

"Is anybody else hungry?" asked Miri.

"Starving," said Len.

"The Golem don't eat," said The Golem. "How far Kentucky?"

"We're like nine hundred miles from the lovely town of Wagner, Kentucky," said Len, who had already explained the geography repeatedly and was beginning to wonder if The Golem had a touch of OCD. "And the Save Our History's

Future rally isn't for two more days. We've got plenty of time to eat lunch. Although . . ."

He glanced in his side mirror. The same nondescript American-made sedan had been behind them for the last ten minutes, maintaining a steady, respectable distance the whole time.

Which, admittedly, was how a highway worked.

But still.

"I'm thinking we should get off the grid for a while," he continued. "We just fled the scene of a congressman's death. In a car we don't own. That *is* owned by people who were . . . I dunno, possibly in open conflict with that congressman over a multibillion-dollar deal? About a piece of land they own and he's gonna be found dead on?"

"That's a good point," said Miri. "But also, I'm very hungry. Like, I don't care. I'll eat anything. Except Arby's."

"My uncle Josh lives in Talbot County, Maryland," Len mused. "That's not too far out of our way. I think we should crash with him tonight, just to be safe."

"Is it *off the grid*?" asked Miri. Len couldn't tell if she was mocking him, but he wouldn't have blamed her. It was hard to believe that life had afforded him honest recourse to employ the phrase.

"The grid would need a bloodhound to find this guy. When I was a kid, he was some kind of fancy lawyer, but he got disbarred. Then he sued his own firm over the disbarment and got a ton of money. So by like fifty, he didn't have to work another day in his life, and he was kind of done with people. He built a cabin deep in the woods, by a little lake, and he's been there ever since, fishing and hiking and distilling his own gin."

"So . . . he's an alcoholic?" said Miri.

"No, no," said Len. "I wouldn't say that at all. He's more of a drunk."

"And a recluse."

"He's self-sufficient."

The nondescript American sedan flashed a turn signal, slipped into the fast lane, and cruised past. Len scanned the bumper stickers: *My Other Car Is a Broom, Something Wiccan This Way Comes, Get a Taste of Religion—Lick a Witch.*

If it was an undercover cop, she was way the fuck undercover.

"All right," said Len. "How 'bout we eat, then head to Uncle Josh's. If I can remember how to get there."

"How long has it been?" asked Miri.

"The last time I visited was in college. So, like twelve or thirteen years. I kind of almost burned his house down."

"Why you fail?" The Golem asked.

"I wasn't trying to burn it down. It was an accident. I'm sure he's forgotten about it by now."

"He's not going to freak out?" said Miri.

"About what, him? I mean, we'll see. But he's pretty unflappable. Unless you burn down his house. Or drink all his booze. I also drank all his booze."

"That also accident, dickhead?" asked The Golem.

"That was deliberate. I was going through a breakup. It's a long story."

The Golem patted Len's shoulder, none too gently but probably as gently as he could. "Nobody wanna hear," he said soothingly.

Stalwart of Justice

The zinc-alloy statue of the Honorable Harrison Grandfield Pettibone that graced the plaza outside the courthouse was eight feet tall and stood atop a six-foot polished granite base. It depicted the legendary civic leader known as the Hanging Judge standing astride the scales of justice, his eyes deep-set and penetrating, a rifle slung across his back, a horsewhip in his right hand and the hooded mask he had worn as Supreme Inquisitor of the Wagner Chapter of the Venerable Order of the Knights of Southern Rectitude clutched tight in his left.

Judge Pettibone, born half a mile from this very monument in 1855, was the youngest son of Wagner's largest landowner. At its peak, the Pettibone plantation produced more than a million pounds of burley tobacco a year, and though the business became less profitable as labor condi-

tions grew less favorable, the Pettibones' place in the firma-
ment of Western Kentucky's social order remained secure.
Young Harrison graduated from the University of Louisville
in 1875, whereupon he returned home to "read the law"
under Judge Sanford Rodgers. Upon his certification by the
state bar association the following spring, Pettibone de-
clined offers from firms in Lexington and Bowling Green in
favor of establishing himself as a sole practitioner in
Wagner—a decision owing largely to the fact that he had
become engaged to a local girl, Susannah Abernathy, the
daughter of a prosperous horse breeder.

His father-in-law-to-be, Calamandous Abernathy, is
credited with ushering Pettibone into the Venerable Order
of the Knights of Southern Rectitude, a social club with
chapters across Kentucky, Tennessee, and Arkansas and a
mandate to uplift the Christian family and celebrate the vir-
tues of Southern culture—all of which were under pernicious threat by the nascent franchise rights of Black
freedmen, now deemed human beings in the glaucoma-
murked eyes of the law.

Pettibone's vociferous embrace of the Knights' activist philosophy both accelerated his ascent through the strata of the
legal community and helped prevent a handful of youthful
miscues—an out-of-wedlock child sired upon a fifteen-year-
old Black housekeeper, an accidental fire that destroyed Wagner's oldest house of worship, an honor duel after an accusation
of cheating at a game of chance that resulted in the maiming of
an unlucky schoolteacher—from derailing that rise.

By the age of twenty-five, Pettibone had been elected to
the bench by the good citizens of Wagner County—a position he would not relinquish until his death, forty-seven

years later—and appointed Grand Inquisitor by his fellow Knights. This put him in the unique position of serving as both judge and executioner; he could in effect choose on a case-by-case basis whether to mete out a sentence legally or extralegally, in judge's chambers or beneath the great vault of the sky, in God's own sacrosanct theater of justice.

Pettibone proved himself a great proponent of judicial restraint; in most situations, rather than overburden the court system or the taxpayers, he preferred to simply roust those who had committed offense from their beds, burn their houses to the ground, and hang them from the neck until dead. He and the Venerable Order of the Knights of Southern Rectitude held the deterrent effect of such direct action to be far greater than any trial by jury, even if the outcome was the same—which, in Pettibone's courtroom, it usually was.

The fruits of their labor were remarkably sweet: despite the fact that Blacks comprised more than a third of Wagner's population—and were essential to its economic viability, as most of them continued to hire themselves out as sharecroppers on the same lands they had formerly worked for free—not a single Black man added his name to the town's voter rolls for the next thirty years. And when the century turned and Chicago's factories crooned their siren songs and the Blacks commenced to leave in droves, the Venerable Order of the Knights of Southern Rectitude congratulated themselves on a job well done, a line held fast, and turned their attention to combating the creeping, triple-headed threat of international communism, the Jewish menace, and the ludicrous notion of women being granted the right to vote.

The statue, inscribed around the base with the epithets
A STALWART OF JUSTICE, A GENTLEMAN OF THE SOUTH, and
A MAN OF FAITH UNDIMMED, had not been commissioned
when Judge Harrison Grandfield Pettibone died, of mouth
cancer, in 1927. Rather, the Wagner County Board of
Trustees—which still counted a Pettibone and an Abernathy among its number—had allocated the funds in 1954, at
the first meeting held after the United States Supreme
Court handed down its ruling in the case of *Brown v. Board
of Education of Topeka, Kansas*. It was a moment of great
upheaval, and the trustees decided that the citizenry needed
moral guidance—a reminder of the values upon which this
community had been founded and upon which it stood still.

What better way than to force all who sought justice to
gaze up at the Hanging Judge's strong-jawed visage and
know exactly what they could expect?

But now—now the town he loved had lost its way,
thought Officer Chadson Nutebridge, gazing up at the
statue. The Board of Trustees had caved to a bunch of whiny
woke crybabies with no local standing whatsoever, community college kids over in Paducah whose Jew civics teacher
had given them an assignment to research the local monu-
ments. Using those kids as pawns to undermine Christian
society and push his globalist agenda—what else was new?

What did surprise Nutebridge was how fast the trustees
had gone all bitch-like and mealy-mouthed. Suddenly Judge
Pettibone had a *complex legacy* that needed to be *reexam-
ined*. Next thing he knew, they were talking about some
bogus community review process, when nobody from the
goddamn community had said boo in the first place. But
that was America these days—go outside to smoke a ciga-

rette, and you might come back in to find your history erased, your culture canceled, and little Johnny telling you he wanted to piss sitting down from now on.

Officially, the Hanging Judge was only being taken down temporarily, for routine maintenance. But Nutebridge knew how this went. There'd never be an official announcement. Just the old *out of sight, out of mind*. Another American hero sacrificed to appease the libtards, suckling at the teats of the Jews.

Unless people like him took a stand.

Nutebridge gazed up at the smooth, hard folds of the hood in Judge Pettibone's fist. The real thing was preserved behind glass in Scott Abernathy's rec room. The Grand Inquisitor of the Venerable Order of the Knights of Southern Rectitude didn't wear a hood anymore, except once a year when the boys went camping and enacted a few of the old rituals their daddies and granddaddies had passed down.

The truth was, Chadson Nutebridge didn't really need a hood. Not when he had a police uniform.

Nutebridge finished his coffee, looked at his watch, and saw that it was nearly time for morning roll. He hopped in his squad car, drove the two blocks to the police building, grabbed a cruller, and refilled his World's Best Dad travel mug on his way into the briefing room.

The entire department was there—not just the six cops on day duty, but the eight who were off, and not just the day sarge but the night sarge and the district commander.

Nutebridge grinned. The story had broken.

He slid behind a desk, pulled out his phone, and jumped on 4Chan.

"White nationalist websites like *The Daily Stormer,*

Frontal Assault, and *I Hope You Like Germans Too* picked up the *New York Times* story last night," the day sarge, Braxton, was saying, a constipated look on his stupid face.

Oh shit dude! typed Nutebridge. *We're in IHYLGT!!*

"The Department of Homeland Security sent over new estimates," Braxton went on. "They're saying five hundred to a thousand marchers, and a small number of counterprotesters."

U fuckrs ready to kick some counterpotester ass? responded Hyland, who was sitting six feet away.

hellz 2 tha yes wrote Carthage, the youngest kid on the force and a third-generation Knight.

please let BLM come bro, from Blanchard, the twenty-year vet and champion deadlifter standing by the window. *My dick is hafrd just thinkinhg about it.*

Spoke to my cuz last night. Hyland again, typing one-handed as he spit tobacco juice into a Gatorade bottle. *He said VOKSR Fayetteville is rolling 20 deep. They all got tents but need places 2 camp . . . GRimey?*

U bet wrote Marshall Grimes, who had a forty-acre spread outside of town. *I'll throw in a bonfire too.*

Brax couldn't find his ass with both hands, wrote Nutebridge, as the sergeant began outlining the peacekeeping strategy.

cuck cuck goose wrote Blanchard, and got a round of laughter emojis.

hey hows this for a slogan, typed Nutebridge, eager to keep the hahas going. *JEWS WILL NOT REPLACE JUDGE!*

Yessssss, from Hyland.

lmbo, enthused Grimes.

Blanchard replied with a GIF of Larry David saying *pretty, pretty, pretty good*—his go-to.

Carthage fired off a string of emojis: fire, biceps, crying-laughing face, scales of justice, hammer, eggplant, wolf. Who the fuck ever knew what that kid was talking about?

Nutebridge thumbs-upped each response, then remembered his cruller and took a big sugary bite.

The King of the Woods

It was night by the time they reached Talbot County. Miri was not sure she had a job anymore, and wishing she had not elected to eat at Taco Bell.

Hey, she'd texted Basam, with two percent battery life left on her phone. *I've got a stomach bug. Had to close up early last night. Been sick all day.*

That's funny, he texted back immediately, as if waiting to pounce. *Because you're not at your apartment.*

Crap, thought Miri. What do I say?

She asked Len.

"Tell him you went to your girlfriend's, so she could take care of you."

Miri must have looked unsure.

"He doesn't know you have a girlfriend, right?"

"I *don't* have a girlfriend."

"That's why it's a great lie. You're distracting him with new information."

"Why would I go to my girlfriend's and get her sick too?"

"Because you're a selfish asshole."

"Or because my bathroom is down a flight of stairs and I basically share it with seven Yemeni guys."

"Don't overthink it," said Len. "Just send the text."

She typed it out, pressed Send—and her phone died.

Had the message gone through? Had Basam replied? Did he think she was ignoring him?

Miri opened the glove compartment, hoping there was a charger, and instead found herself staring at a five-pound bag of miniature Butterfinger bars.

Of course. The Admor was diabetic.

"Oh shit," said Len. "Jackpot. Guess we don't have to stop for dinner."

"I'm not eating candy for dinner, and neither are you."

They passed a Next Exit sign: Sbarro, Taco Bell, Arby's, Chick-fil-A.

"Pick your poison," said Len. "And keep in mind that Chick-fil-A hates gay people, which is too bad because it's definitely the least disgusting option." He glanced over. "Wait—you don't keep kosher, do you?"

"Yes and no," said Miri, the answer sounding ridiculous even to her.

Len waited for her to elaborate, so Miri didn't.

Forty minutes later, she had consumed two hard-shell chicken tacos and purchased a phone charger that plugged into the SUV's cigarette lighter, and the consequences of her own ethical failure had been made manifest. Sometimes Hashem's designs were incomprehensible, the arc of His justice too long to perceive on a human scale. Other times it moved as swiftly as the line at the Easton, Maryland Taco Bell, or the body's digestive process.

"If you lie about being sick," Miri said, resting a hand on her roiling stomach as she shared her findings, "you get sick."

"I don't think you're giving Taco Hell enough credit," said Len, shoveling curly fries from Arby's into his mouth as he drove. "But don't worry. We're one exit away."

The Golem had been quiet for some time. Miri turned and peered into the darkness. "Is he asleep?"

"The Golem don't sleep," came the reply. "Also don't talk when nothing to say."

Miri checked her text thread with Basam, and once again the screen showed the ellipsis that meant he was typing. It had been appearing and disappearing for the last hour and a half, implausible though it seemed that Basam had spent that time writing and deleting and rewriting the perfect sympathy text, or the perfect *You're fired* text, or the perfect *You're fired and evicted* text.

Len turned off the highway and onto a country road, the headlights revealing nothing but blacktop and double yellow. Either Basam had given up on crafting his masterpiece, or they had entered a no-service zone.

"You can see a billion stars out here," said Len. "It's nuts."

"This is the first time I've ever been outside of New York City," Miri told him.

Len, to his credit, said nothing.

After a few minutes, he turned onto a dirt road, and flipped on his high beams. They were in the woods now;

Miri could feel trees all around her, even if she could barely make them out. They loomed and pressed together like buildings, the forest as dense in its own way as Brooklyn.

Len buzzed down all the windows and warm air rushed inside, and then so did a tapestry of sound that was like nothing Miri had ever heard—buzzing and clicking and chirruping and rustling. Her astonishment must have shown on her face, because Len grinned at her.

"It's like a fuckin' symphony, right?"

"But what *is* it?"

"Nature. Talking to itself."

That was strangely poetic, Miri thought, as she began to pick out individual refrains and time signatures, distinguish the percussive interjections of one bug from the uninterrupted hum of another, the frictive underlay of branches moving in the breeze from the frenzy of animals scuttling or fighting or foraging beneath.

Maybe people were different out here. Maybe even Miri.

Len piloted the SUV at five miles an hour, the speed the road allowed. Miri leaned as far out the window as she dared, catching glimpses of night sky where the trees gave way, and sure enough—stars like she had never seen and never bothered trying to imagine. It made her feel as if she had been living under glass, as if the bubble surrounding the Sassovs was a literal thing, an upturned filthy fishbowl, a cataract that smudged the heavens' majesty. She wanted to cry and breathe as deeply as she could, so she did both. The symphony seemed to breathe with her, as if the forest were one single organism and Miri was a part of it, and in that moment she was moved to ecstasy by the melody that issues forth from every creature in the whole of creation, and felt that every atom of her body was suffused with God.

"Holy fucking shit," said Len. "That wasn't here before."

He stopped short, and Miri looked where he was looking: down a side road that forked off the main and ended thirty feet away, where a Range Rover was parked on a gravel driveway before a boxy modern glass-and-poured-concrete house, yellow pin lights illuminating various points of architectural interest: a terrace wrapped around a second-story bedroom, a massive wooden front door that looked stolen from a medieval castle, an empty kitchen that almost definitely had one of those stoves with the giant red knobs and a refrigerator disguised as a wall.

They both stared at it, and the song of the forest grew quieter. Finally, Len drove on.

Another two minutes down the road was another turnoff, another hulking house. The driveway sat empty.

"Uncle Josh cannot be happy about this," said Len.

A slow quarter mile and half a dozen houses later, the road bifurcated and a hand-painted sign explained that Lakeview Lane lay to the left, Waterfront Road to the right.

Len shrugged and blew a breath through pursed lips. "Fuck if I know."

The Golem, who had not spoken in an hour, leaned forward into the space between Len and Miri's seats and broke his silence. "There is old story about man who have to choose between two road. One way is okay, but other way have monster with knifes for teeth. And his asshole shoot fire."

"Taco Bell," said Len.

"Two men guard roads. One always tell the truth, and one always never tell the truth, and you can only ask one question."

"You ask 'Which way would that fucker over there tell me to go,' and then you go the other way."

"How you know that?"

"Everybody knows that." Len twisted in his seat. "Why, is it supposed to be like some metaphor for the Jewish people or something?"

"Everything metaphor, shmendrick," The Golem said, and withdrew back into the darkness.

Len spun the wheel and turned left—then slammed his foot against the brake as something darted across the road, thirty feet ahead.

"What the hell was that?"

"I don't know," said Miri. "A deer? A bear? Are there bears here?"

"It didn't move like a bear. It moved like a person."

"Too big," said The Golem. "Open door. The Golem gonna find out."

"Absolutely not," said Len. "Let's get to my uncle's."

"Can just break door," The Golem pointed out.

"Why do you care what it is?"

"The Golem's job is protect. Also, need some action. Been sitting on ass listening to bullshit all day."

"Fine. Hurry up." Len pressed a button and the locks flipped. "Who protects us from the protectors, that's what I want to know."

"That interesting philosophical question, dickhead," said The Golem, clambering out onto the road. He flared his nostrils and turned his head slowly, a few degrees at a time.

"What are you, tracking it?" asked Len, as The Golem got a bead on his quarry and dashed off.

The woods swallowed him up in moments, but Miri could hear the crashing and snapping and bludgeoning of trees and twigs and logs, the obliterating thud of his every footstep. It was chaos set to a beat.

And then—a scream of terror so abject and desperate it had to be human. Miri sprinted toward it.

"Don't hurt me!" she heard as she stumbled blindly down the trampled path The Golem had left in his wake, and Miri shouted back:

"Don't hurt him!"

Her shirt caught on a branch and Miri felt it lacerate her skin, scrape a gash across her arm just below the biceps.

Whatever, it didn't matter. Someone up ahead was pleading for his life. She tore free and ran on.

And then the forest opened up just slightly, as if each of a dozen trees had taken one step back. The break in the canopy let in the moonlight, and the moonlight shone down on The Golem.

His foot rested atop the chest of a writhing, wheezing beast—an ape of some kind, but unfathomably large, eight or nine feet from head to toe, with long brown fur, a barrel chest, a face just as expressive as her own—and Miri was no wildlife expert but she knew this didn't make one fucking lick of sense. No ape this big existed, and no apes at all lived in this forest, this continent, this hemisphere.

The whole scene was so utterly confusing that it took her a moment to remember she'd heard a voice, a man, begging for help.

"Where'd he go?" she asked.

The Golem cocked his head at her as if he didn't understand the question.

"Where who—" he began, and that was when Len charged into the clearing. He stopped beside Miri and looked from The Golem to the supine, struggling ape-thing.

"What the fuck?" he said. "Is that fucking *Bigfoot*?"

20

The Black Hand

Len sipped from his Mason jar and winced. This stuff was terrible, and he could practically feel it making him go blind. But if he'd ever needed a drink, it was right now.

"Yeah, no, I strongly disagree," he said. "In no way is that the only logical response to the situation."

Uncle Josh poured them each another two fingers from what looked like a brass watering can, then topped off Miri and The Golem, neither of whom had touched their portions.

The cabin was more or less as Len remembered—books and VHS tapes overflowing from handmade shelves, dried flowers and salamis hanging from the rafters, giant framed 1960s Italian advertising posters that had seemed sophisticated and fun when they'd hung in the high-rise South Loop bachelor's condo of a rich Chicago litigator but felt somehow apocalyptic here.

Uncle Josh, meanwhile, looked like shit. He'd lost most of his hair, except for a gray fringe that started at the crown of his head and hung halfway down his back, as did his beard. His arms were still wiry and strong, but his stomach was enormously bloated—less like a gut than a hot water bottle filled to the bursting point.

He was clad in nothing but his boxer shorts and a pair of knee braces, and seemed perfectly comfortable entertaining his nephew, a strange woman, and a golem in this state of undress. The bigfoot costume lay inside out at his feet, all its secrets laid bare: the rough hand-stitching where the flaps of bear hide were joined, the smears of dried blood, the foam inserts to extend the arms, the jerry-rigged stirrup system that added nearly three feet of height to the legs and looked like an absolute bitch to walk in.

"I lost my paradise," he said. "I used to walk naked in these woods. Swim naked in the lake. Sleep naked under the stars. And then"—Uncle Josh snapped two thick fingers—"everything changed. They parceled it up and sold it off. I don't hear the forest anymore. I hear construction crews. I hear Bob the investment banker telling his wife to flip the steaks. There's jet skis on the lake. It's everything I came here to get away from."

"So naturally, you started dressing up like Bigfoot and terrorizing your neighbors."

"They terrorized me first."

"The game plan being what, exactly? That if they think the missing link is wandering the woods, they'll pack up and leave?"

Uncle Josh shrugged, and Len saw moisture rising to the corners of his eyes. "I don't know. It's just . . ." He sighed. "It's something to do."

"The suit is very impressive," said Miri.

"Thank you. It's been a labor of love. And hate."

"Did it ever occur to you that you could get hurt?" Len asked. "Or shot?"

"Did it ever occur to you that *you* could get hurt or shot, running around with a fucking golem?"

"It definitely occur to The Golem to hurt him or shoot him," said The Golem.

Uncle Josh dropped his elbows onto the table, peered across the room at him, and said, "You, my friend, are a miracle."

He had to be close to blacking out, thought Len. He'd probably been drinking this shit all day, and after a few sips Len could barely control his eyeballs.

This was not a healthy man.

"You know," Uncle Josh said, "a lot of these fuckers around here, they hate Jews."

"Stop it," said Len, terrified of where this was going.

"Seriously, The Golem," Uncle Josh went on, ignoring him. "I get called a filthy kike or a Christ-killer practically every day."

"He's kidding."

"These guys stand around their barbecue grills drinking German beers and planning pogroms, I swear to God."

"Seriously, knock it off."

The Golem strode over and looked down at Uncle Josh. "You maybe most craziest person The Golem ever met. Tell you what. Pick one house and The Golem destroy."

"No!" said Len and Miri together.

"That's easy," said Uncle Josh. "Bob Brubaker. The fucking adobe shit palace that looks like it should be a New Mexican drug rehab center. You probably passed it on the way in."

"How is this protecting the Jews?" demanded Len.

The Golem shrugged. "He Jewish treasure."

"Let me tell you a story, Lenny," said Uncle Josh, "about your great-grandfather." He waved a hand loosely at Miri and The Golem, his elbow an increasingly wobbly fulcrum. "He calls me his uncle, but I'm really his dad's first cousin." He swung his finger around to Len. "What do you know about Martin Bronstein?"

"Not that much," said Len, happy to be talking about anything besides the cataclysmic destruction of property. "He pushed a pushcart in the Bronx or something."

"Your father only saw them a couple times a year. But me, I grew up a twenty-minute subway ride away. We visited every weekend when I was little. And then when my grandmother died, Grandpa Marty came to live with us. We shared a room for a while.

"One day my dad came home with a Woody Allen album. We all sat down around the stereo to listen, and after about ten minutes Grandpa Marty gets up from his chair, grabs his cane, hobbles over to the turntable, grabs the record, breaks it over his knee, and walks out of the room.

"That night, when we're both lying there in the dark, I ask him why he did it. And he says *All this namby-pamby, scared of his own shadow, complaining about everything—that's not what a Jew is.* Then he turned on the lamp. *Come here, Sonny Boy,* he says. *Go under the bed and take out my suitcase.* So I do. And what's Grandpa Marty want to show me?"

Uncle Josh paused, as if expecting a round of guesses. When none were forthcoming, he poured himself another drink.

"His pistol. I'm eight, sitting there holding a sixty-year-old gun. And it's fucking loaded. *Put it back away, Sonny,* the old man says. *And don't ever touch it again.* Then he lights up his pipe. I'm sitting there on the floor, trying not to piss myself, thinking about what my parents would do if they knew there was a loaded gun in my room.

"And he says *Go ahead, Joshie. Ask me.*

"*Zayde, why do you have a gun?*

"And he says to me, *Have you ever heard of Joe Toblinsky?*

"*No, Zayde.*

"*Johnny Levinsky?*

"*No, Zayde.*

"*Charley the Cripple?*

"*No, Zayde.*

"He puffs on his pipe, and he says, *Those three ran the Yiddish Black Hand. If you wanted to sell ice cream on the Lower East Side? Manufacture seltzer? Run a livery stable? You paid them. And if you didn't pay, Sonny Boy? Then I came around with my pistol.*"

Uncle Josh nodded at Len. "I said exactly what you said. I said *I thought you had a pushcart.* And Grandpa Marty said, *Where do you think I kept my gun?*"

The Golem picked up his Mason jar of moonshine and sniffed at it.

"You don't eat or drink," Miri reminded him.

The Golem shrugged. "What worst that could happen?" He raised the jar, like a doll's teacup in his mitt, and threw the liquid down his gullet.

He shrugged. "Not have tam-vortslekh."

"Taste buds," said Miri.

"The Yiddish Black Hand," said Len. "It sounds like a joke."

"It sounds like a joke because nobody remembers who we used to be. Including us."

"Maybe we don't want to," said Len. "Maybe we've evolved."

"Nobody evolves," said Uncle Josh.

"Neither of you has any idea what you're talking about," said Miri. She scowled at Len. "Did you already forget my brother? The Shomrim?"

"Yeah, but that's different." He turned to Uncle Josh. "Hasids."

"We walked around the city with big fat dicks in our trousers," said Uncle Josh.

The Golem crushed his Mason jar to smithereens with his fist, and everyone jumped.

"Sore subject," said Miri.

"I assume you're quoting Marty," said Len. "Because you don't live in a city, and you're not wearing pants."

"He said it. I never forgot it."

"Well, it's very evocative."

"Years later I went online and found a Black Hand price list some informant had given to the cops. A murder was five hundred dollars. A nonfatal shooting was a hundred. Poisoning a horse was thirty-five."

"I bet nobody tried to Jew them down," said Len.

He looked around the room, immensely proud of himself. But Miri was stone-faced, The Golem was still brooding over his lack of a shmok, and Uncle Josh had passed the fuck out in his chair.

21

The Lies of The Golem

It was not entirely true that The Golem had, until now, been made exclusively by prophets, priests, and rabbis.

To put it another way, he was lying.

Or perhaps he had chosen to forget.

The Golden Age of Judaism in Spain lasted from the middle of the eighth century to the end of the eleventh, in the region then known as Al-Andalus. Under Muslim rule, the Jews were a protected class, subject to additional forms of taxation and barred from martial training, but considered fellow People of the Book and allowed to flourish. And though some historians contend that "Golden Age" is an imposition of seventeenth-century Jewish propagandists whose nostalgia for Muslim rule was informed by the boot of Christianity under which they were currently living, and a more accurate name might be the Intermittently Less Shitty

Age, there is no doubt that this period represents a rare la-cuna in which whimsical massacre, forced conversion, and sudden exile did not loom as daily possibilities.

The Jewish people were permitted to practice their religion and even maintain their own courts; they in turn ad-opted many Arabic and Islamic customs, such as the ritual washing of the hands and feet before entering a house of worship. And they contributed deeply to the rich and so-phisticated life of the region as scholars, doctors, botanists, mathematicians, and especially translators.

The poetry and history and philosophy of the world, thus far segregated into discrete linguistic spheres—Arabic, Hebrew, Greek, Aramaic, Latin—was being transformed, at long last, into a shared body of knowledge. It was a project that heralded a newly cosmopolitan age, and the Jews were uniquely qualified to partake in it. Not only were they past subjects of empires that spoke all these languages, but they had often been barred from owning land and thus confined to precisely the kinds of liminal, urban professions that re-quired multilingualism: merchantry, medicine, artisanal work, and yes, fine, moneylending.

The political and cultural nexus of Al-Andalus was the Caliphate of Cordoba, an ancient port nestled between the mountains and the highest navigable point of the Gua-dalquivir River that had blossomed into the world's most cosmopolitan city. Jewish scholars from across the diaspora flocked there, drawn by an invitation to establish an inde-pendent academy, and by the early eleventh century it ri-valed the Babylonian schools at Sura and Pumbeditha as the world's greatest site of Jewish learning.

It was at this great gathering-place of the wise and learned that Yapheth ha-Levi worked as a stable-hand, feeding and watering the many horses housed at the academy and sometimes assisting the cooking staff in meal preparation.

One day, a week before the High Holidays, with the academy short-staffed due to an outbreak of influenza, Yapheth found himself pressed into duty serving a group of visiting rabbis in an outdoor courtyard overlooking the mountains. These men were mystics, of the sort who would go on to write the Kabbalah in centuries to come, and as Yapheth filled their cups with wine and replenished the trays of local cheeses, which they were consuming as if they had not been fed in days, he lingered to listen to their rapid-fire conversation, conducted in Hebrew laced with occasional phrases of Arabic as well as one, perhaps two, additional languages Yapheth could not identify.

The topic of the conversation—one might even say the argument—was golems: by whom and out of what and for which purposes they might be made, whether any of the rare and conflicting accounts of their creation was credible or whether they were all fabrications, mistranslations, metaphors gone wrong. The discussion veered from law to scripture, then moved on to nephilim and dybbuks, and before long Yapheth was lost and the rabbis were drunk and the sun was setting and the meal was ready to be laid out in the dining hall.

But a flame had been kindled in Yapheth that burned all through the night.

The next morning, he entered the library and requested several obscure tracts the rabbis had mentioned, two written in Hebrew and one in Aramaic, saying that he was acting on behalf of a Babylonian scholar whose name Yapheth invented on the spot.

That afternoon, he claimed to feel a stabbing pain in his stomach, and departed from the academy several hours before sunset. He hiked up through the forest until he reached the rocky outcroppings at the base of the mountain, which were riddled with caves.

Yapheth selected a deep, narrow one, lit the candle he had brought with him, sat down, and began to read. He was not gifted with languages; he was gifted with horses. And he neither spoke nor read Aramaic.

But he had also never experienced an epiphany like the one he'd had last night, as bracing as a plunge into a frigid lake. Perhaps once in a lifetime, or once in a century, did a humble stable-hand see what the great scholars could not. Yapheth was the instrument of the Lord, and he understood what he had to do.

He spent the next twelve years trying and failing. He read the tracts until he knew them backward and forward, filled satchel after satchel with mud from the banks of the great river and carried it to his cave and molded it into the shape of a massive man and moistened the figure with water every day so that it did not crack and crumble.

His sense of purpose never wavered. The epiphany remained undiminished, faultless, perfect in his mind. And so when at long last Yapheth succeeded in animating his golem, and The Golem sat up and shook his head as if clearing it after a long nap and demanded, in Aramaic, a language Yapheth now spoke, to know his purpose here, Yapheth was able to explain with sublime clarity.

"You are here to discover the secret One True Name of God, the Absolute Hundredth Name that no man has ever known—more powerful than the forty-two letters of the Ein

Sof the scholars have extrapolated from the permutations of the Tetragrammaton, and holier than the seventy-two seventy-two-letter names of the Shemhamphorasch, derived from the three seventy-two letter verses of the Book of Exodus."

"Huh?" said The Golem.

"You shall find it so that I may speak it and summon my creator and look upon his face," Yapheth said, as a dying candle flickered behind The Golem and cast monstrous, lurching shadows across the walls.

"I do not understand," said The Golem. "This is the work of a scholar. I am a brute."

"No," said Yapheth, overbrimming with delight, for this was the elegance, the logic of his revelation. "That is the great mistake! You are a creature made through the manipulation of the alphabet, just as Adonai made the world! Your true purpose is to be the key that unlocks the door behind which He stands. This is the reason the greatest scholars and the holiest men have failed: they did not realize that they could not discover the name, but only bring about the being who could."

"Are you a rabbi, a priest, or a prophet?" asked The Golem.

Yapheth thought for a moment, then said, "Perhaps, if it please Adonai, I am a prophet."

He rose and began to assemble the many texts he had acquired in anticipation of this moment.

"Here are all the holiest books of our people," he said, splaying one hand against the Talmud and the other against the Torah, then springing up to retrieve the Mishnah, the Tosefta, the Midrash, the Sefir Yertzirah, the Mekhilta, the Avot of Rabbi Natan.

"I cannot read," said The Golem.

"You will learn," Yapheth assured him. "This is your destiny. To find the path to the path, and then the path, and then the name."

The Golem shrugged. "You're the prophet," he said.

"You shall devote yourself to this task from dawn to sunset every day," the stable-hand explained. "I shall come each evening, when my work is done, and look in on you."

"Is there no one trying to kill Jews?" The Golem asked.

"Not currently, no."

"How about a dam that needs fixing?"

"You must trust me," said Yapheth. "You mistake yourself for a brute just as we mistake ourselves as creatures of mere flesh, bound to this celestial plane. But look at me: I made you. I am become like to the Lord."

The Golem did not argue, and the days of study began.

A year passed and he learned to read both Hebrew and Aramaic, slowly and with frequent miscues.

Yapheth was not discouraged. It had taken him twelve years to unlock the secrets of The Golem; it might well take twice that long for The Golem to unlock the greatest secret of the universe.

On the third month of the fifth year, Yapheth was hiking to the cave when he came across a striking rock formation, twice his height, composed of seven boulders stacked into the shape of a pyramid.

"Did you pile up those rocks?" he demanded when he reached the cave.

The Golem nodded without looking up from the Talmud, open on his lap.

"Why?" asked Yapheth.

"I do not know," The Golem said.

"Never do it again," Yapheth commanded, his voice taut, and The Golem nodded again.

"How many times have you read that book?" Yapheth asked.

"Seventy-four times, and not at all," said The Golem.

Another nine years passed, and The Golem began to spend his days simply wandering the woods. He would return to the cave when the sun dipped low and the light grew golden, and study for a few hours, his tireless eyes running along the tiny lines of text, and wait for the revelation the prophet was so certain would come.

If Yapheth was correct, The Golem reasoned, then it did not matter whether The Golem read for fourteen hours a day or two.

And if he was incorrect, it also did not matter.

The Golem was immensely proud of this feat of reasoning. Never in his long, mottled existence had he even attempted such a thing.

In the eighteenth year of fruitless study, a tiny green shoot began to sprout from The Golem's shoulder, where a seed had managed to lodge. The Golem found that this pleased him. He allowed it to grow, until a thin vine of greenery trailed down his back.

Yapheth said nothing of it.

On the nineteenth day of the eleventh month of the twenty-second year, The Golem did not return to the cave. Yapheth found him standing immobile, a quarter mile away, near a stand of beech trees.

"What are you doing?" he asked, but The Golem did not respond.

"Stop this foolishness at once," Yapheth shouted.

The Golem remained perfectly still.

Yapheth began to panic. He had never read a word regarding the sudden unresponsiveness of golems—but then, he also had no knowledge of any golem who had remained animate for so long, or been assigned such a task as this.

He tried everything he could think of to restore The Golem: every permutation of the spells and holy words that had surrected him, every mystic incantation that seemed even remotely relevant. As the days became weeks and then months, Yapheth began simply opening various holy books at random and reading out the words upon which his eyes chanced to fall.

Throughout it all, The Golem remained utterly still, utterly patient, utterly himself. He waited for the stable-hand, who was not and had never been a prophet, to give up.

On the last day of summer, Yapheth sank to the ground before The Golem and cried. He had never married, never fathered children, never seen the sea.

The sea wasn't even that far away.

Yapheth disappeared, and The Golem despaired.

Then he returned with the entire contents of the cave, every book and tract, wrapped up in a bundle of cloth and slung over his back, and The Golem sensed that he was soon to achieve his goal.

Yapheth arranged the books into a kind of staircase, ascended carefully to the top, and reached up with the palm of his hand.

He erased the aleph from The Golem's forehead, turning truth to death and The Golem into the statue he had pretended to be.

Bodies Are Just Bodies

The first ray of sun woke Miri and she opened her eyes and tried to sit up, only to find her cheek stuck to the leather couch by a paste of dried drool and her head throbbing like it had her heart inside.

Is this what it's like to be young? she thought.

She used a palm to spatula her face free, rose, and had a look around.

Len was passed out on the floor, the bigfoot suit draped over his midsection like a blanket. Miri surmised that Uncle Josh had woken up, covered his nephew—cousin—and then staggered to his bedroom, from which wet, ursine snores were emanating every few seconds.

The cabin smelled like alcohol, salami, and body odor, and The Golem was nowhere to be seen.

Which seemed . . . bad.

Miri pulled on her sneakers, considered rummaging through Uncle Josh's kitchen for coffee, decided against it, and stepped outside into the glowing light, the dewy air, the world made new.

Wherever The Golem was, he could wait. This was too beautiful not to savor. The pressure in Miri's head eased as though someone had spun a valve, and Uncle Josh seemed suddenly less like a psychotic old crank than a genius. She walked a few paces and stared down at the glinting lake from atop the gently sloping bank.

Something breached the placid surface with a tiny splash, and Miri's head jerked toward the sound. She scanned the water for the disruptor, but it was already gone, a thing of the past, not so much as a ripple left behind.

Out here, a million tiny sounds added up to stillness. Why, then, in New York, did a million tiny sounds add up to cacophony? Was it the sounds themselves? The way the city held them? The way they fitted together?

Miri's gaze skittered across the water, picking out patterns of shadow and light. She imagined standing here all day, watching the shifting play of breeze and ripple. Then doing it again the next day, and the next, until those rhythms began to live in her.

Then she imagined some putz on a jet ski carving up the water, the peace, and felt another shock of understanding for Uncle Josh.

Miri walked down to the edge of the lake. It lapped the toes of her sneakers, so she took them off, balled up her socks, double-cuffed her jeans, and stepped into the cold, soft water.

She stood there a moment, acclimating, then returned

to shore, stripped off her jeans, and strode into the lake until she was waist-deep, half below it and half above it, a satisfying symmetry. The bottom, packed firm in the shallows, was squelchy here.

This had turned into a ritual.

It had never before occurred to Miri that one might invent a ritual rather than merely inheriting it, enacting it. A vista as wide as this lake was opening inside her, where before there had only been a keyhole.

She splayed her palms out parallel to the water, then plunged her hands in to the wrists and took another step forward. She was going to keep going until the water reached her mouth, it seemed to Miri now, and she wished she'd taken off her shirt and bra. She didn't want to wade all the way back to shore, so she pulled them off, dunked them in the lake to give them weight, then balled them up together and heaved them onto the shore.

Three more steps, and the water reached her rib cage. Miri's legs were warmer than her torso, and she wondered if it was because they'd acclimated or because the lower stratum of the lake absorbed more heat than the top.

She turned her head left and right, taking in the breadth of the lake. It looked very different once you were inside it. She bookmarked the thought.

Then something in the periphery of her vision moved, and Miri startled, lost her footing for a moment, remembered she couldn't swim, and wondered what the fuck she was doing in this lake.

The Golem was sitting a hundred feet away, behind a stand of reeds, only his head and the tops of his knees breaching the waterline. Miri's eyes had slid right over him.

Now he stood, the water sloshing off his back and shoulders. The lake hid him from the waist down, creating the impression that he was gliding as he walked toward her.

He covered the distance quickly, and all of a sudden Miri remembered that she was naked. She crossed her arms over her breasts, then bent awkwardly at the knees, trying to find a way to submerge herself to the neck without leaving her feet.

Hold on, she thought. What am I doing? Do I actually care if The Golem sees my tits?

She did not, any more than she cared if men saw her calves or God saw her hair. That wasn't Miri, it was the life she'd left behind—and that was when it hit her.

This lake was a mikveh.

If there was anything Miri had looked forward to about her preordained, inescapable life as a married woman—anything she had not dreaded—it was the ritual of the mikveh, the purifying bath. Married women took one, alone or together, after they bled. Her mother had never missed a month. Men went every Sabbath; her father had never missed a Friday.

Miri took a deep breath, pinched her nostrils closed, and dropped beneath the water. It filled her ears, canceled out the world above. She counted off the seconds—one, two, three, four—then rocketed back onto her feet and dropped her hands to her hips.

The Golem stood beside her, impassive.

The two of them gazed out at the far shore for a moment, just a couple of naked beings standing quietly in the water. Someplace overhead, a bird called and another bird replied.

"So what are you doing in this lake?" asked Miri.

"Same thing you doing."

"How long have you been out here?"

"The Golem leave when everybody fall asleep. Place smell like giant asshole."

"You didn't . . . break any houses, did you?"

The Golem shook his head. "That just drunk talk."

"You were drunk?"

"No, like . . . talk-to-drunk talk. The Golem not so . . . how you say. Gringleybik."

"Gullible."

The Golem nodded. "Uncle Josh not first drunk who want The Golem to destroy a village."

"Yo!"

Miri turned and saw Len standing at the top of the bank. "We should go," he called. "I packed the car."

"What do you mean, packed it?" said Miri, crossing her arms over her chest. She *did* care if Len saw her naked. That was gross. "We don't have anything."

"Just, you know, provisions." He paused. "I'm feeling a lot of FOMO right now. I think I'm gonna jump in too. But after that, we should go."

"Fear of missing out," Miri explained to The Golem, proud that she knew, as Len stripped down to his boxer shorts.

The Golem squinted at her in a way that felt judgmental, and Miri considered how stupid the phrase probably sounded to a five-thousand-year-old crisis monster.

Len belly-flopped into the lake, stirring up a bloom of silt.

"Oh, man," he said, turning and floating on his back, "that sure cleans out the cobwebs."

His stomach was fish-belly white, his chest hairless except for little wiry snarls that thatched his nipples. None of this was information Miri wanted, but that was on her. Bodies are just bodies, she reminded herself.

Len stood, slicked back his hair, and started climbing up the bank.

"Come on," he said, pinwheeling an arm. "We really should get on the road."

Miri stayed put. She didn't like being herded and she wanted to say goodbye to the lake and the woods on her own terms, whatever those might turn out to be.

"What's the rush?" she asked.

Len pulled his jeans up over his soaking wet legs.

"I want to get out of here before Uncle Josh wakes up and realizes I stole his bigfoot costume," he explained. "For his own good, obviously."

"Obviously," said Miri.

"Best case scenario, he gets arrested. *Best* case."

"I'm agreeing with you."

"Oh. Okay." A drop of water fell from his hair to his clavicle. "I don't feel great about it, to be honest."

"Well, you shouldn't," said Miri. "But more than one thing can be true."

"We going or we talking?" asked The Golem, stomping past them both.

23

Good for the Jews

By noon, they had crossed into Enemy Territory, which was a nickname Len had just invented for West Virginia. He was inclined to take his foot off the gas as infrequently as possible, but Miri, who had slept through the day's first pit stop for gas and coffee—the two liquids equally palatable at this particular Kwik-Fuel, in Len's opinion—was pushing hard for lunch at a classic American diner.

"You're gonna be disappointed," Len warned her. "It won't be like in the movies."

"I can't eat fast food again. I want to sit down."

"You're sitting down right now."

"I want a waitress in an apron to come over with a pot of coffee and say *Can I warm you up, hon?*"

"That's weirdly specific."

Miri shrugged and keyed a search term into her phone.

"Is this waitress young and cute?" Len said, trying to tease her.

"She's old and bitter. Here we go. Old Kounty Diner. Twenty miles away."

"Let me guess—they spell 'county' with a K."

"How did you know?"

"They love unnecessary K's out here. It's a way of signaling their affiliation with the Ku Klux Klan."

Miri threw him a sideways glance that Len knew meant she was pretty sure he was kidding but didn't want to ask.

It wasn't until the two of them were sitting in a cracked red leatherette booth, holding cheap white ceramic coffee mugs with a stripe around the rim that matched the leatherette, that Len realized Miri had insisted on this foray into fine dining because she wanted to talk out of The Golem's earshot.

"I know I'm the one who showed him the video," she was saying. "But I didn't think it through. I just wanted to get him away from them." She toyed with a sugar packet, and Len waited for more.

"What do you think he's gonna do when we get there?" Miri asked after a moment.

"Hopefully what we tell him to."

It had sounded stupid in his head, but he'd said it anyway, in case he was wrong and it was reassuring, or struck Miri as plausible. But it sounded even stupider out loud.

"What are you basing that on?"

"Very little."

She gave him a withering look, as the waitress—who was not in uniform, and did not seem interested in warming anybody up, but was certainly old and possibly bitter—came over to find out what they wanted for lunch.

Len ordered the BLT. Not only was it an all-time top-five sandwich, it might also throw any interested parties off the scent of his Judaism. There weren't many parties of any kind in evidence—a couple of geezers eating pie at the counter, a mom and her two young kids making a mess of a booth in the rear—but you never knew. And anybody could be lurking in the kitchen, frying up the bacon. Or standing outside, clocking the SUV with the New York plates and the tinted windows and *Sweet Lord Jesus, did something just move in there?*

Pancakes, eggs, and fries for Miri. Good for her. Do it right, girl.

"I have no money, by the way," she said, when the waitress walked away. "I work in a bodega."

"That's okay. I did say I would pay you to translate."

Miri smiled. "That was, what, six weeks ago?"

"Seems like it, huh?"

A plate smashed against the floor and they both jumped.

"Maddox! You be a gentleman!" the mom in the back booth remonstrated her three-year-old.

"You know," said Len, "we don't have to take him to Wagner. We could say the march got canceled. Or I could just drive someplace else. There are any number of ways to play it."

Miri brightened. "I hadn't thought of that."

The waitress returned with their meals, and Miri doused everything with maple syrup and dug right in.

"You were wrong," she said. "This is perfect."

Len took a bite of his sandwich. It was maybe the best

BLT he'd ever tasted. "Goddamn," he said. "Give it up for Kool Kountry Kitchen. Who woulda guessed?" He pushed his plate into the center of the table and pointed at the other half of the sandwich. "Wanna try?"

Miri shook her head. "It's one thing to be a big gay shonda. It's another to eat pork."

Len watched her saw a jagged bite of pancake and shove it in her mouth.

"Let me ask you something," he said. "What do you want him to do?"

"What do you mean?"

"When we get to that rally. *If* we get to that rally. What are you imagining?"

Miri swallowed and dabbed her lips with a napkin.

"I want him to scare them. And I want the world to see it. And then poof, he gets away. Disappears to fight another day. To appear where he's least expected. So they're *always* afraid."

"You've thought about this," said Len, trying to sound neutral but feeling obscurely betrayed. Why did everybody but him have a secret agenda—a secret agenda that cast Len in the thankless, brainless role of golem chauffeur?

"I don't want any more death. But what good is a golem if nobody knows he exists? And after all these thousands of years, who's even heard of golems? Just Jews, right? Maybe it's time to change that."

"Well, I mean, Jews and the . . . Jew-adjacent."

"But the average gentile? The people in this restaurant right now?"

"Should we take a poll?" He caught the waitress's eye, and before Miri could stop him, Len beckoned her over.

"Don't," Miri hissed, but Len was feeling just aggrieved enough not to care.

"Can I warm you up, hon?" the waitress asked, brandishing a fresh pot.

"Sure." Len held out his mug. "Hey, can I ask you something? Do you know what a golem is?"

She nodded as the coffee sluiced down the molded plastic chute. "From *Lord of the Rings*."

Len smiled, then figured he should follow up. "And, um . . . do you think he was misunderstood?"

The waitress warmed Miri up, then put a hand on her hip and gestured philosophically with the pot.

"He's a tragic figure, in my opinion," she said.

Maddox flung a saucer to the ground and the waitress sighed, gave them a little wave, and walked over to sweep up the shards.

Len chomped into the second half of his BLT, feeling victorious and like an asshole. Miri swiped some fries through a pool of syrup, a pensive look on her face.

"How about this," she said after a moment. "We take him someplace nice and private, someplace we can look him in the eye, and we ask him what he's gonna do. Or no, we tell him—we say *Your job is to scare them and then vanish. Like Spiderman. So they know there's someone out there who protects us.*"

"That sounds more like Batman than Spiderman."

"Whatever. If he says yes, we take him to Wagner. But if he objects in any way, we do what you said. Get lost. Lie. Figure a way out of it."

"How do you think he's going to handle that?"

"He's been through worse."

"If I had to guess," said Len slowly, "I would say The Golem is not going to be content popping out from behind a tree and saying *booga booga* to a bunch of people we already told him want to kill the Jews. To say nothing of the whole vanish-into-thin-air part of your plan." He made quotation marks in the air. *"Plan."*

"Well then we're in luck, because then we don't have to go to a white nationalist rally in Kentucky," Miri said, and popped the last three French fries into her mouth.

Len studied her for a moment, waiting for Miri's facade of nonchalance to crack. But she was resolute about keeping her head down and finishing her eggs, and he ran out of patience.

"So now we're trying to invent a superhero?"

Miri laid her fork down. "If I've learned anything since I left the Sassovs and joined the real world, it's that people love superheroes."

"Yeah, in *movies*. Shit, Miri—people already believe that George Soros controls the world economy and Jews have secret space lasers. You really think—"

Len broke off, snarled in his thoughts. He was down to his last bite of BLT, and he was severely tempted to order another one.

"You really think that would be good for the Jews?" he finished weakly.

24

Who Do You Trust

"Y**ou smell like pig,"** The Golem said when Miri and Len returned to the car.

"I ate some bacon," said Len. "But it's okay. There were a couple of rabbis in the restaurant, and they said a blessing over my BLT."

The Golem reached forward and flicked Len's ear with his finger. Len bellowed and clapped his hand over it.

"Ow! Fuck! That really hurt!"

"Joke not funny," The Golem said.

"Remind me never to take you to a comedy club."

Len pulled out of the lot and drove slowly up the country road. Miri pulled down her sun visor, and Len watched her watch The Golem in the mirror, tried to gauge from her face what she saw in his, whether The Golem noticed that they were not heading back to the highway. But Miri's face revealed nothing, and The Golem seemed to have slipped back into standby mode.

Five minutes slipped by. Scrubby forest lined both sides of the road, and they saw only two other vehicles—a pickup and an empty half-sized school bus, both traveling in the opposite direction.

Len looked over at Miri and raised his eyebrows in a question.

She nodded, and spoke quietly.

"Wherever."

They rounded a bend and an empty parking lot came into view, thistles bursting through the cracked concrete. In the middle was a long, boarded-up one-story building whose faded sign suggested that it had once been Anna's Farm Stand, and at the rear was a stately tree, the canopy high and wide enough to cast half the lot in shadow. Behind the tree was a field of weeds, and then a forest.

Len parked next to the building and opened his door. "Why you not pee at diner?" The Golem demanded.

Miri turned to look at him. "We're stopping because we want to talk to you," she said evenly. "Let's all get out and stretch our legs, okay?"

The Golem grunted and unlatched the trunk, and then all three of them were standing in the barren lot.

"I actually do have to pee," said Len. "Hold on."

He walked off behind the farm stand and stared up at the tree, its upper branches swaying slightly in a breeze that was nonexistent down here on the ground, as he relieved himself.

He turned the corner in time to see The Golem pick up a jagged chunk of concrete that must have weighed seventy or eighty pounds and whip it casually across the lot and the road. It tore through the air like a meteor hurtling toward earth and disappeared soundlessly into the foliage beyond.

The Golem picked up another, larger than the first. The lot was littered with them; somebody had jackhammered something to pieces and then lost interest in the disposal.

"Stop!" said Len. "Why did you do that?"

"Bored," said The Golem, somehow managing to look like a petulant child. "Also, gotta stay in shape." He wheeled and shotput the slab in the opposite direction. It flew high into the sky and crashed into one of the outermost branches of the massive tree with a resounding crack, and both plummeted to the ground.

"You actually *don't* have to stay in shape," Len said, feeling petulant himself. "You just are the shape you are."

"The Golem not mean literally, shit-for-brains." He poked a bit of rusty rebar with a toe. "Anyway, what you want talk about?"

Len walked over to Miri, stood next to her, and crossed his arms. In another life, the two of them were a married couple about to confront their thirteen-year-old son about the dime bag they'd found in his dresser.

"We want to be clear on what happens when we get to the Save Our History's Future rally," he said. "We want to go over the plan."

The Golem picked up a four-foot length of rebar and javelined it at the sun, missing narrowly.

"Plan is, The Golem gonna kill everybody," said The Golem.

"Well, shit," said Len.

"No," said Miri, shaking her head. "No. That's definitely not what we want you to do."

"The Golem gotta protect the Jews," The Golem said. "This not hard concept to understand."

"It will be bad for us if you do that," said Miri, stepping closer to him. "Please. You have to believe me—it will be better if you just scare them."

The Golem snorted in derision. "You real student of history."

"She doesn't have to be," said Len. "She's telling you about the world *right now*. Because you're only *three days old*."

The Golem waved dismissively, in a manner oddly identical to the way Len's grandmother used to do it.

"World is world," The Golem said. He pointed at Miri. "Besides, you not from right now. You from play-acting like it eighteenth-century Ukrainian shtetl. Du klingst oys glat lekherlekh. Host gornisht keyn batsiyung tsu der virklekhkayt. And nobody wore those fur hats in the summer."

"You want to get shot again?" asked Len. "You wanna end up in another ditch? Or"—His mind raced to generate a suitably terrifying scenario—"in some dungeon, getting experimented on by a bunch of government scientists who wanna figure out how they can control you? And clone you? And use you as a weapon?"

It was, Len suspected, more or less the plot of an *Uncanny X-Men* comic book run from his youth. But it didn't matter. The Golem didn't know that.

"No," he said. "The Golem not want that. But The Golem also not afraid."

"You could be a superhero!" Miri blurted. "You'll do more for the Jews as a, a—"

"Mysterious vigilante?" offered Len.

"As a mysterious vigilante than you ever could as a, a—"

"Murderous goon?"

"Yes," Miri said. "Exactly. Thank you."

It was a weird time for politeness, but Len was nothing if not gracious.

"Think nothing of it," he heard himself say.

We've all lost our minds, he thought.

"I want the whole world to know about you!" Miri said. "Every Jew-hater. Every bigot. It's *their* turn to be afraid!"

Too much, thought Len.

"Look," said The Golem. "The Golem like you." He turned to Len. "You too, dickhead. But you both not know shit about The Golem. What The Golem tell you, first thing, right away? The Golem is for time of crisis. The Golem do his job, then fuck off until next time there is job. The Golem not, how you say, langtsaytike farentferung."

"Long-term solution," translated Miri, her voice breaking.

The Golem nodded. "Also, The Golem not supposed to be famous."

"Says who?" demanded Miri. "What if—"

Len put a hand on her arm, and Miri went quiet.

"Who would you listen to?" he asked The Golem. "Who do you trust? Obviously not us. That's fine." He slid his phone out of his pocket and brandished it at The Golem. "But there must be someone. So you tell me who it is, and I'll fucking call them. And if they sign off on this, then great. We're off to Kentucky." He glanced at Miri to see how she was feeling about this spontaneous and ill-considered deviation from the plan, and found her staring intently at a spot on the ground three feet in front of her, like a cat about to throw up.

"But if they say no," Len continued doggedly, "then that's it. End of the line. I erase the aleph and you fuck off until there's a job for you to do. Or—we drive back to Brooklyn. I'll even drop you on Menachem Sassov's doorstep, if that's what you want. Your choice. So. Who do you trust? The Grand Rebbe? Waleed? Uncle Josh? Larry David? Because they're all gonna tell you the same thing."

"Larry David," said The Golem.

"I can't actually call Larry David. How about Waleed? You said Waleed was cool."

"Waleed cool, but Waleed not wise. Larry David remind The Golem of Hillel."

"You knew Hillel?"

"Little bit. Funny, for rabbi. Beard have a good smell. Invent shnitkes."

"Sandwiches," said Miri, typing furiously on her phone.

"Right!" said Len with a manic intensity, thrilled to be talking about anything besides turning Wagner, Kentucky, into a bloodbath, and afraid to find out what was going to happen when he shut his trap. "Why's it called a Hillel's Sandwich, anyway? It should be a Sandwich's Hillel! The Earl of Sandwich lived like eighteen centuries later, and he only quote-unquote *invented* that shit because he was a degenerate gambler who wanted to eat dinner without leaving the poker table. Plus, his sandwich was just bread and ham. You know what a shitty sandwich that must have been? Meanwhile, Hillel was rocking roast lamb, bitter herbs, charoset—basically a full-on shawarma. But what is he remembered for? The Golden Rule. You wanna talk antisemitism, there's your fuckin' antisemitism right there."

He glanced at Miri, willing her to jump in, just as Miri looked up from her perusal of the internet.

"I think I found a number for his manager," she said.

25

Shlimazel Promise

"Will you listen to him?" Miri asked, the number all cued up.

"Depend what he say."

"That's not listening," said Miri. "You have to promise that if by some miracle I'm able to get Larry David to talk to you, you'll actually do what he says."

"That shlimazel promise." The Golem waved a slab-like arm at Len. "He could say to stick whole head up dickhead's ass."

Len looked disgusted. "Why would he do that?"

"The Golem not know what kind of weird shit Larry David into."

"Fine," said Miri. "If he makes a bizarre sexual request, you're free to ignore it. But on the specific matter of killing people at the Save Our History's Future rally, will you listen?"

"Why would sticking his head up my ass be sexual?" Len asked. "That's where your mind goes?"

"I'm dialing," said Miri. She walked away from both of them, pressed the green button, and brought the phone to her ear.

"Hold on."

She turned to see Len jogging toward her. "Maybe I should talk to him?" he said.

A pang of self-doubt twanged through her as the phone rang, and she almost handed it over. Then Miri stopped herself. Why should she? In what possible way was Len more qualified to explain this situation to Larry David's manager?

"Fuck off," she said, as the switchboard operator answered with the management company's initials and asked how he could direct Miri's call.

"Cass Finkelstein's office, please," said Miri.

"Tell his assistant you're from, um . . . Universal," hissed Len. "But also, don't be you, be your assistant. Say 'I have Miri Whatever Your Last Name Is for Cass.'"

Miri nodded. This seemed like prudent advice. Len was absolutely more qualified to make this call.

"Should I make up a name?" she hissed back.

"What is your last name again?"

"Apfelbaum."

"Right. No, that's perfect. You sound like somebody he's never heard of who works at Universal. Like a midlevel exec who just got promoted because somebody got MeTooed."

"Cass Finkelstein's office," said Cass Finkelstein's assistant.

"I have Miri Apfelbaum for Cass," Miri said as crisply as she could, suddenly wishing she had peed before making this call.

There was a tiny pause. Miri imagined the assistant typing her name into some database of people who mattered, where it would return no results.

"From Universal," Miri added.

Another pause. She shouldn't have said that. It sounded wrong, even to her.

Fuck, she mouthed at Len.

"Let me see if I can grab him," the assistant said, and Miri's eyes went wide.

"Yesss," said Len, pumping his fist.

She put the phone on speaker, so he could advise. "Please hold for Cass," the assistant said.

There was a click, and then, "Hey, Miri," said the affable voice of, presumably, Cass Finkelstein. "How's tricks?" He sounded to her like a very tan sixty-year-old Jew wearing an expensive watch. There were a lot of them on TV.

Miri took a deep breath and switched the phone into her other hand, which was slightly less sweaty.

"So, uh . . . you know what a golem is, right?" she began.

"Sure," said Cass. She heard a squeak, like he was reclining in his chair. "But I gotta tell you, Miri, the golem market is dead."

"No," she said, "Listen. I'm— I don't work at Universal. You don't know me. But I'm standing in a parking lot in West Virginia with a giant, actual, real-life golem, and he's about to go on a rampage and murder dozens, maybe hundreds, of antisemites, and the only person who can stop him, the only person he might listen to, is Larry David."

There was a long, airless pause, and then Cass Finkelstein's rich, sonorous chuckle exploded from the speaker.

"That's fucking *amazing,*" he said. "I actually think Larry will love this. And he's been looking to do a feature in Q4. This is a feature, right? Janice, are you still on the line?"

"I'm here," said the assistant.

"Can we—can you ping Larry? He's home. We were just texting."

"Yes, Mr. Finkelstein," said Janice.

"I'm not— This isn't a pitch," said Miri. "It's a matter of life and death."

"Incredible. Do it just like that."

Len leaned close and whispered in Miri's ear. "Tell him we need to switch to Zoom."

"Can we switch to a Zoom?" Miri repeated.

"Sure," said Janice, chipper. "I'll send an invite now. Can I just grab your email?"

Miri heard herself spell it out.

"Great! Let me grab Larry, and we'll see you in conference." Janice hung up.

The Golem whipped a hunk of concrete at Anna's Farm Stand. It skimmed across the entire length of the roof like a stone across a pond, gashing great holes.

"Would you please knock that off?" bellowed Len.

"Actually," said Miri, "that might be a good thing to show Larry."

She checked her email and found the Zoom invitation.

"Okay," she said, beckoning The Golem. "Come here. We're gonna talk to Larry David."

"Finally," said The Golem.

He ambled over just as Janice admitted Miri to the Zoom room. Cass Finkelstein was there, looking much as Miri had anticipated, and a moment later so was Larry David. He was sitting on a patio, or a deck. Dappled sunlight fell across his face, and there was a tantalizing pink wisteria vine behind him. The photogray lenses of his eyeglasses were half in the sun and half in the shade, one side clear and the other opaque.

"Larry," Cass was saying, "this is Miri. She just knocked my socks off. That's all I'm gonna say—I'll let her take it from here."

"Nice to meet you, Miri," Larry said loudly, as if he knew she was very far away.

"Hi," said Miri. "Nice to meet you too. I'm, uh—"

Len crowded in behind her, and waved. "Hi, Mr. David. Len Bronstein. I'm a huge fan."

"Oh, well, thank you," said Larry. He smiled a patient smile, a wise smile, a smile Miri believed Hillel might have smiled. "I've gotta confess," he said, "I have no idea what this meeting is about. Are you two in a parking lot?"

"We are," said Miri. "This meeting is about the fact that Len made a golem. This is him."

She angled her phone up at The Golem, trying to get his face in the frame and keep the sun out of it, despite the fact that it seemed to be situated directly, and barely, above The Golem's head.

Larry leaned in, and squinted at his screen.

"Are you serious?" he said. "You're telling me that's a real golem? Like, made out of mud?"

"I actually used sculpting clay," said Len.

"But it's a prop," said Larry David, as if reassuring himself. "I mean, to state the obvious. Because what is this, the Middle Ages?"

"No, no," said Len. "He's real." He turned to The Golem. "Go ahead, say hi. Show Mr. David you're real."

"The Golem real," said The Golem.

"Check this out," Len said, and nudged The Golem. "Go ahead. Take out the door or something."

The Golem shrugged, ambled a few paces, and hefted a trapezoidal piece of rubble with the remains of a metal pole stuck in it. He waited until Miri's phone was trained on him, then tossed it through the air like a sledgehammer, end over end. It smashed into the front wall of Anna's and the entire structure collapsed, boards falling in on each other as if a black hole had suddenly been born inside the abandoned farm stand.

"That was . . . lovely," said Larry David. "But I guess I'm not clear on what any of this has to do with me. I already have a contractor."

"You're the only person he'll listen to," Len said, taking the phone. "He learned English by watching *Curb Your Enthusiasm,* and—"

"See, Cass?" said Larry. "Aren't I always telling you the show is educational?"

"—and now he wants to go to Kentucky and kill a bunch of white supremacists. And we—"

"Great," said Larry David. "Terrific. Mazel tov."

"Hold on," said Miri, aghast.

"No, really," said Larry. "Those *Jews will not replace us* pieces of shit? I'm all for it. He should kill as many as possible. Maybe rip their heads off—do you rip heads off?"

"*Can* rip heads off," The Golem said.

"Well, I don't want to tell you how to do your job, but maybe some of them, you rip the heads off and then fuck the necks," Larry said. "What the hell, right?"

"This shmegegge forget to make The Golem a dick,"

The Golem said, jerking a thumb at Len. "So not really possible, Larry."

"Having a dick is a mixed blessing, honestly," said Larry. He shrugged. "So forget the neck-fucking. Cass is looking at me like I'm disgusting anyway."

"No, no," Cass assured him. "Love the neck-fucking. This is why they pay you the big bucks, pal."

"I was just being colorful. Regardless. Big thumbs-up from me, Golem. *The* Golem. I don't love *The* in front of a name, to be honest. That never leads anywhere good. Until now, maybe. Who knows? Anyway, good stuff. Let me know if there's anything else you need, okay?"

"The Golem knew it," said The Golem, turning to Miri and Len, less triumphant than smug. "Deal is deal. Let's go."

"Fuck this," said Len. "I'm not driving you. I don't care what Larry David says."

"You make promise." The Golem's face darkened and he took a step toward Len, who dropped the phone and tore ass in the direction of the road.

Miri winced as her screen shattered against the ground. "Hello?" she heard Larry David say. "I can't see anything."

The Golem picked up another piece of concrete.

"Do not be beyzer lo-yutstlekh," he called out. "Stop!"

Len stopped, but not because The Golem had convinced him.

He stopped because he was in the middle of the road, and a West Virginia state trooper's patrol car had just screeched to a halt to avoid running him over.

26

The Middle of the Road

"The hell you doin' in the middle of the road?" the state trooper demanded, stepping out of his vehicle and taking a couple of hard-charging steps toward Len with his hand on the butt of his gun. "You on drugs or somethin'?"

"No," said Len, and then it occurred to him—clarity slicing through the surge of catecholamines cascading into his nervous system like a bodysurfer diving through a breaking wave—that if this khaki-hat-wearing constable of the peace turned his head another forty-five degrees to the left, he was going to see something infinitely more worthy of drawing his service weapon on, and the shit was going to hit the fan.

"I mean—yes!" Len amended. "I'm on a ton of drugs, and they went *that* way!" He pointed a finger at the forest, and opened his eyes as wide as he could, suddenly feeling like he actually was on a crazy-making dose of something, maybe methamphetamine. If Miri and The Golem had any sense at all they'd managed to scamper out of sight behind the giant tree by now, and it took all the discipline Len had not to check, to stay laser-focused on his imaginary runaway drugs.

The trooper pulled his gun. Instinctively, Len raised his hands.

This was going great so far.

"Turn around! Put your hands on your head and interlace your fingers!"

"Okay! No problem!" said Len, and he turned slowly, sneaking a look at the parking lot.

Aw, shit.

Miri was nowhere to be seen, but apparently The Golem had decided that Len could be both his antagonist and a Jew worth saving.

The Golem was large; he contained multitudes.

He crossed the lot with giant strides, flat feet slapping the ground, and the trooper's eyes ticked toward the sound.

"What in the holy hell!"

His whole body, and the revolver that had become its extension, swiveled to confront this newer, far more present danger.

The Golem kept coming, no slower and no faster, and Len knew what was going to happen before it happened, because he read copiously about cops and their training and how they learned to identify and respond to threats, which was basically to kill them as quickly as possible. And if most cops found twelve-year-old Black boys terrifying, then a nine-and-a-half-foot craggy-faced gray walking nightmare was definitely not going to reap the benefits of any department-mandated tactical de-escalation workshop.

The report from the first shot made Len jump. He saw The Golem's left shoulder jerk back where the bullet hit, but that was the only discernable effect, except that his expression changed from grim and resolute to grimly amused.

Len realized that his own hands were still woven together atop his head, and dropped them to his sides just as the trooper fired again. This bullet didn't seem to hit The Golem at all, despite his having halved the distance between them, which spoke to a mounting panic response, a failure of marksmanship commensurate with the same epinephrine-soaked overload Len himself had experienced just moments ago.

Before the trooper could fire a third time, The Golem opened a clenched fist and slapped the gun out of his hand. It skittered away down the road, cleaving remarkably, if accidentally, close to the double yellow line.

The Golem raised his other hand and Len braced for gore, but The Golem merely flicked out a finger and knocked the trooper's stiff, broad-brimmed hat from his head, then bent forward at the waist and flared his nostrils and took a good long sniff.

The trickle of piss that ran down the trooper's leg seemed to jog his mind, or at least his mouth.

"What are you?" he asked, voice wobbly with something that, if Len hadn't known better, he might have mistaken for reverence.

The Golem stared pointedly at Len while he answered. "Depend what *you* are," he said, then lifted his leg, pulled back his knee, and kicked the trooper backward into his car so hard that the impact crumpled the door and the rear side panel around his body and held it in place.

Blood oozed through his uniform, and he wheezed wetly. Len was no coroner, but he supposed the kick had crushed the guy's rib cage, and maybe shards of rib were stabbing him in the heart, or puncturing his lungs, or both.

The Golem glared at Len, whose breath was coming in ragged gasps.

"You safe now, dickhead," The Golem declared.

"Uh, no I'm *not*," said Len. "And neither are you, because you just killed a cop, and we're—"

"The Golem not kill cop."

He walked over, squatted before the mangled patrol car, and grabbed it by the undercarriage. With a grunt, he sprang up like a powerlifter and flipped the vehicle and the trooper through the air. The side mirrors caught and threw off blinding flashes of sun as they spun, rapid and inscrutable as a secret code. The car cleared the tree line and crashed down somewhere beyond, in a four-thousand-pound riot of metal and plastic and bone.

"*Now* he dead."

The Golem wiped soot and black grease off his hands and onto his thighs, then turned and walked back toward the parking lot.

Miri was standing on the far side, beneath the lush, indifferent tree, looking very small.

Len put on a burst of speed and cut in front of The Golem.

"Come on, man," he said. "Let's just go home."

"The Golem not have a home."

He didn't break his stride, forcing Len to dodge out of

the way and then continue his appeal as he flitted in and out of The Golem's field of vision, like a fucking gnat.

"Look, mission accomplished, okay? You sniffed out a Jew-hater and you killed him."

"Can still smell stench in nostrils," The Golem said, and if he'd been grim before he was grimmer now, and Len knew it was futile to try to change his mind.

"Here's the deal," he said, and instead of keeping pace with The Golem he just stopped moving, and to his surprise The Golem did the same and turned and looked at him and waited. And for perhaps the first time ever, it felt to Len as if The Golem was not looking past him or through him, but at him and into him.

Len did not expect to feel so moved by this, or so scared. There was a lump in his throat, a drop of sweat sliding ever so slowly down the underside of his arm. The idea of tricking The Golem seemed both impossible and dangerous now. Honesty didn't feel particularly safe either, but maybe safety was always an illusion.

"I'm sorry," he said. "But I can't do this. I won't. And if you try—"

The Golem rushed him, and before Len could finish his sentence he was airborne, limbs akimbo, flying upward, the warm air rushing past.

His feet were still below him; he had not been man-handled or thrown carelessly but lofted with great precision. It was still terrifying to see the Golem shrink beneath him and the boughs of the tree rush past, but this knowledge made it less so—and when he landed with an ass-rattling thump atop a broad branch, twenty or thirty feet off the ground, at the juncture where it connected to the great thick trunk, Len's first thought was *Yeah, seems about right*.

The Golem craned his neck and shaded his brow with the flat of his palm. He spoke quietly, but the words rose.

"Sorry too, dickhead."

He dropped his head, walked to the SUV, and opened the trunk. "Time to go," he said.

Len couldn't see Miri, but her voice sounded out like birdsong.

"I don't know how to drive. That's . . . why I haven't driven. And I wouldn't take you even if I could."

"I guess that's that," called Len. "Game over, The Golem. Now how about you get me down and we talk this out like grown-ups and figure out another way to help the Jews, huh? Hello?"

The Golem made a low, angry sound deep in his throat.

He snatched the bigfoot suit out of the trunk, splayed it on the ground like a bearskin rug, and hunched over it for a moment, poking and prodding, his back like a massive sea turtle.

"The hell do you think you're doing?" shouted Len.

But he knew.

Miri stepped into view, and squinted up at him. She knew too.

"Are you all right up there?" she asked.

"Oh, yeah. I'm great. Ten out of ten, would recommend."

"Just sit tight. We'll figure something out."

"I'm sitting as tight as I can," Len said, trying to sound chill but also kind of annoyed.

They both fell silent as The Golem sat down with his

legs kicked out in front of him, like the world's largest pre-schooler, and billowed the suit across his lap.

Then, with a degree of care, patience, and fine motor skill utterly at odds with everything Len had seen from him thus far, The Golem proceeded to remove all the padding from the costume—everything Uncle Josh had built to turn a six-foot drunk into a nine-foot sasquatch.

When he was finished, he stood, stepped into the suit, and zipped himself up from knee to armpit.

Len peered down at him. The fringed fur hung over The Golem's feet and hands. The head was snug across his bulbous dome, but the eyeholes seemed to match up.

It was a stunningly convincing fit, if you completely disregarded the conventional meaning of the word convincing.

The Golem shook out his limbs, rolled his neck, and walked off into the woods without a goodbye or a backward glance.

27

The Monster and the Little Girl

The Golem trudged through the forest for hours with no idea where he was going, trampling saplings and crushing half-rotten logs. He thought nothing and felt nothing, his mind an empty vessel. Even his senses were dimmed—his nostrils covered by the mask, his vision tunneled.

He thrashed into a clearing and stopped.

Sitting on the forest floor, inside a three-sided house made of sticks, was a small girl wearing a long black T-shirt and holding a ham and cheese hillel on white bread with mayonnaise.

The part of The Golem's brain that anticipated things came back online, just in time to be wrong when the girl didn't scream or flee, but merely blinked at him.

"You were in my dream," she said.

"What happen in dream?" The Golem asked.

"You came to my lair and I gave you tea. This is my lair. You want some tea?"

"The Go—" The Golem began, then stopped himself.

"The Bigfoot not drink tea," he said.

The girl stood up and held out a chipped ceramic cup.

"My dreams always come true. Take the tea."

The Golem bent and accepted the cup. It was empty. "You weird kid," he said.

"I'm a witch," said the kid. "Tell me a story."

"The Bigfoot not have time," said The Golem. "Thanks for tea."

"Tell me a story and I'll use my powers to help you," pledged the witch.

"This happen in dream?"

"Yes."

"How you help The Bigfoot?"

"Your name's not The Bigfoot," said the witch. "That's just your disguise. But you never tell me who you really are."

"Real name The Golem. You probably not heard of."

The witch stamped her foot against the ground. "I just said, you never told me. Now you've messed up the dream."

"That not The Golem problem," said The Golem, and prepared to walk on.

The witch flung her own ceramic teacup at The Golem. It hit him just below his furry knee and landed facedown on the mossy forest floor. "If you don't tell me a story, I'll use my powers to fuck your shit up."

"Could stomp you like ant, witch."

"But you won't." The witch sounded confident.

"The Golem's shit already fucked up. Need to get to Kentucky."

"I know," said the witch.

"You lying," said The Golem. "You not witch. You just weird kid acting witchy. Ikh bin nit geboryn gevorn nekhtn. The Golem not born yesterday. Born *Saturday*."

"Tell me a story, and I promise I'll help you."

The Golem unzipped the head of his costume so he could take a proper look at her—and give her a proper look at him.

The stench of pig hit him immediately, but he smelled past it. There was nothing else there to object to. The witch did not hate Jews.

She was young still.

"What is a golem?" she asked, peering at the new face that had replaced the old.

"Whatever he need to be. Whatever the world make him."

"That doesn't make any sense," said the witch. "That means a golem is nothing."

The Golem shrugged. "Maybe you right. How old are you?"

"Eleven," said the witch. "How old are you?"

"Depend how you do math. You know story of Adam and Eve?"

The witch nodded.

"Only time word golem appear in Torah, it describe Adam after God make him out of clay, but before fill him with breath of life. Mean unfinished thing."

The Golem broke off and furrowed his brow.

"Never try put this in words before," he explained. "It not

like in book, with garden and apple and snake. That steaming pile of bullshit. Or metaphor. The Golem don't know."

He paused again, gathering his thoughts. The witch nibbled her hillel.

"There was moment, when God had just start to breathe breath of life . . . and The Golem not fill up with it and become Adam yet, but also not unfinished thing anymore. Like, in-between moment. But time not exist yet, or human time anyway—just God time. So for all The Golem know, in-between moment last hundred million years. And The Golem or Not-The-Golem see everything at once and gain great mystical understanding of entire universe and five worlds of spirit, all while breath enter lungs.

"Then Adam exhale and human time begin, and mystical understanding vanish, and The Golem vanish. And next time The Golem wake up, world totally different. Totally fucked up. And The Golem totally different and totally fucked up."

The Golem was quiet.

The witch watched him carefully, her blue eyes keen and sharp.

"How that for story?" he asked at last.

The witch grimaced. "I meant like a *story*," she said. "With characters. And a beginning, middle, and end."

The Golem cut his eyes at her. "The Golem never tell anybody that. Not Moses. Not Solomon. Not Larry David."

The witch shrugged, and offered no help.

The Golem sat down heavily beside her, and the house of sticks collapsed. "Fine," he said, and told her another.

This story took place during the Babylonian Exile, and concerned a minor rabbi named Yehezkel ben Yedidya, whose name is lost to history and was largely lost even to the present in which he lived.

This is no slur upon his character. For every rabbi so magnificently pious or learned or original in his theology or prodigious in his writing that he is remembered by future generations, there are thousands who can only hope to provide some measure of guidance and clarity to their congregants, to lead a good Jewish life and inspire others to do the same.

Yehezkel was not among these thousands, either; he belonged to the next stratum of rabbis down. He had no congregation, claimed no august pedigree, did not have the luxury of spending his days in contemplation of the holy books. He was, however, a useful man to know—a man of his time. He could write a contract in such a way that it satisfied both the Jewish and Babylonian authorities. He mediated disputes with cunning, if not wisdom. And unlike the upper strata of rabbis, whose theology was calcified and static, Yehezkel was not only conversant with the superstitions and occult preoccupations of the people—his own and the Babylonians in whose midst they dwelled—but a fervent believer in many. It was mainly on such matters that his counsel was sought, by farmers and merchants and even, on rare occasions, by the great rabbis themselves.

So when Yehezkel's firstborn son died before he could undergo the rite of circumcision on the eighth day of life, Yehezkel's mind went straight to demonology, and he dug up the incantation bowl buried upside down before the threshold of his home, and to his great dismay found it broken into three pieces.

A bowl buried whole did not break of its own accord. Someone had unearthed the protective talisman, with its depiction of the bound demon Lilith at its center and the protective verses spiraling to the edges of the ceramic, destroyed it, and reburied it.

The first seven days of life were a liminal time, a lacuna of great vulnerability to demons, and some enemy had exposed Yehezkel's son unto death.

Yehezkel did not know who this enemy could be, but this was the least of the rabbi's problems. More dire by far was the fact that Lilith only despised children of whom she had reason to be jealous—the half siblings of her own brood. If she had killed Yehezkel's son, the bowl had long been broken, and she had ingressed his home before.

She had taken the form of Yehezkel's wife, Tsipora, and Yehezkel had lain with her and sired a demon-child.

Or she had entered the house in her male guise, known as Lilit, and taken Yehezkel's shape, and lain with Tsipora—in which case Yehezkel's daughter was not his daughter but an unholy thing. If this was so, it would not be revealed until the arrival of her menses. She would begin to crave blood and revile the Torah, and they would have to cast her out.

But that nightmare, should it come to pass, was at least a long time away. There was the present to think of.

Tsipora was pregnant again.

It was a boy, the midwives said. Yehezkel had buried a new bowl, but this alone was not enough to prevent the demon from returning to rob him of another son.

And so on the day the boy was born, Yehezkel made a golem from the mud of the river and the blood of his right hand, and awakened him using the rites he had been taught by his great uncle, a rabbi of equally low pedigree who nonetheless knew some things.

Yehezkel bade The Golem to stand watch outside the house until the eighth day came and the crisis passed.

"What am I to look for?" The Golem asked.

"The danger may take any form," Yehezkel told him.

That night, The Golem killed an ostrich who wandered close to the door, seizing it by the neck and bashing its brains out on a rock.

"I do not think that was Lilith," said Yehezkel in the morning, auguring the entrails. "But you have done well. Rest until evening, for Lilith is a demon of the night."

"I do not rest," The Golem said. "I will continue to keep watch."

"You're scaring my neighbors," said Yehezkel.

"Didn't one of them break your incantation bowl?"

Yehezkel considered this. "On second thought," he said, "walk to the center of the Jewish quarter, and declare that if any man has a quarrel with the rabbi Yehezkel, humble servant of Hashem, let him come forward and it shall be resolved, and his trespasses forgiven."

The Golem did as he was told, and returned to find the rabbi just as he had been, pacing back and forth before the house. The cries of the newborn could be heard from the bedchamber within. He sounded healthy to The Golem.

"No man came forward," he reported. "Though several called out loudly, and said you are no rabbi."

"Lilith has bewitched them," Yehezkel muttered.

That night, The Golem espied a small animal whose

name he did not know digging furiously in the ground with sharp front claws, so he chased it down and stomped it to death. Some hours later, he dispatched another.

"They could have been searching for your incantation bowl," he told Yehezkel in the morning, holding up the mangled corpses, already swarmed by flies.

Yehezkel stared at them with distaste. "Good work," he said, but there was no force behind the words, and though The Golem had done precisely what had been asked of him, he felt that he had failed.

Yehezkel turned to go, then reconsidered and turned back. "What do you know of Lilith?" he asked.

"I know nothing," said The Golem, who was not accustomed to being well informed.

"Lilith was the first woman the Lord made for Adam," explained the rabbi. "But she would not submit to him. She said they were created from the same clay, at the same time, and must be equals. They argued for the whole first day of their lives, and then Lilith spoke the Ineffable True Name of God, which no mortal has known since. It filled her with great power, and she flew away over the ocean. And no longer was she a woman, but a demon, and a mother of demons beyond count, and a seducer of men, and a murderer of children."

The Golem nodded, though none of it quite lined up with what he remembered.

That night the baby forgot how to latch on to the breast and screamed until dawn, and the only living things to set foot anywhere near Yehezkel's property were a trio of drunken Babylonian boys who fled down the road in terror when The Golem stepped into the moonlight.

The next day, a wizened tanner of hides presented himself to Yehezkel and said in a quavering voice that although he was ashamed to admit it, his heart was hardened against the rabbi.

Yehezkel, his left eyelid spasming from lack of sleep, received the tanner warmly and with vast relief. His son was too weak to scream now, but the silence did not portend any rest.

The tanner explained that the rabbi's wife had taken six sheepskins from his stall in the marketplace some years ago, pledging to return and deliver payment, then failing to do so.

"I did not want to bother you, rabbi," he said. "But the truth is, when business slows down to a crawl and I can barely afford to put bread on my table, my thoughts toward you and your wife can be a tad unkind."

Yehezkel barely appeared to be following.

"And for this you destroyed my incantation bowl and invited a demon into my home to violate my wife and kill my child?"

The tanner looked at him aghast.

"I've done no such thing!" he spat. "Are you mad?"

"I'm sorry," said Yehezkel. "I have not slept. I'm sick with worry. And Tsipora, may Adonai keep her and protect her, is very forgetful. And very bad with money."

He tried to pay the tanner what was owed, but the tanner refused. Then he accepted. Then he left.

That night, a ten-foot serpent slithered onto the property, and The Golem tore it to pieces with his bare hands. Yehezkel ordered the beast burned, and since he had not bothered to specify how the ostrich or the small digging varmints should be disposed of, The Golem assumed that at last he had killed well.

Later that afternoon, the baby finally took some milk.

The next three nights were quiet. The baby fed and slept and grew stronger. Yehezkel wept tears of joy and prepared to circumcise his son.

The stars were veiled on the last night of The Golem's vigil. As he peered into the darkness, at the blackest hour of the night, a tendril of fog began to gather along the ground, and then to spin itself up into a kind of sketch of a female form that trailed off just below the knees and elbows, and floated a few feet off the ground.

The woman was clothed only in long tresses of hair that wrapped themselves around her body. Her face was deeply grooved and impossibly beautiful.

The Golem had no doubt that this was Lilith.

She glided toward him, and The Golem prepared to attack.

"Who has drawn me to this place?" she asked, in Hebrew, and The Golem could not be sure whether she had spoken the words aloud, or he had heard them inside his head.

"You are here to kill the baby," he answered in the same language. "And I am here to stop you."

The Golem reached out and grabbed at her with his fists like stone, but there was nothing to touch. Lilith dissipated and reformed and seemed not even to notice.

"I know nothing of a baby," she said. "I am naught but what you see before you: a fog, a shadow, a mist that wanders on the winds and drifts toward the sound of my name."

"Lilith," said The Golem, just to be sure.

"Lilith."

"Seducer of men," recited The Golem, trying to remember. "Mother of demons. Baby murderer."

"I am none of these," said Lilith. "I have no children at all."

This is a trick, The Golem thought.

"I would not need a trick," Lilith replied, so either he had said it without realizing, or she had heard it without speech.

The Golem could feel her intelligence probing him, exploring what was there. The sensation was slight and brief and not unpleasant.

"I am a being of pure spirit and pure disobedience," she said. "We are opposites, you and I. How would you stop me, if I were any of the things men say I am?"

"I could not," The Golem admitted.

"My blessings upon you, and this baby," said Lilith. "They are as meaningless as my curse."

And she was gone.

When Yehezkel and Tsipora awoke at dawn, their son lay on the bed between them, dead, and they began to wail.

After some hours, The Golem entered the house and interrupted their lamentations. He wanted to tell them that their son had died a natural death, believing that this might grant them some small measure of relief.

But Yehezkel refused to let The Golem speak. He cursed his name and beat him with his fists until the knuckles were raw and bloody. He accused him of betraying his master, of conspiring with Lilith.

Finally, he ordered The Golem to kneel before him. And wild-eyed with grief and rage, Yehezkel turned truth to death.

28

Nothing's Free

"**D**o you know about the twelve labors of Heracles?" asked the witch, whose name was Lena, as they walked along a darkening country road, toward her house.

The Golem snorted. "That Greek pretty boy idea of labor like, kill one lion, sit on asshole and drink wine for two years. Capture one boar, sit on asshole and drink wine for two years."

"You knew him?"

The Golem shook his head. "Not really move in same circles."

"Well," Lena continued, undaunted, "think of this as being like the fifth labor, when he cleans out the Augean stables."

The Golem scowled at her. "When you say you gonna

use your powers to help, The Golem not think you mean get him job shoveling shit."

"Nothing's free," said the witch.

They turned off the road and onto a long dirt driveway. The witch slapped away seven mosquitoes in the time it took to reach a low wooden fence that had once been painted white. Set well back from it, across a wide lawn and past a small garden surrounded by chicken wire, sat a low ranch house that glowed a warm yellow inside, and gave the impression that it was settling slowly into the ground.

Inside, a man tipped a can of beer to his mouth and pressed a button on a remote control, and the light grew harsher as the television flickered on.

"I'll go talk to him," said Lena. "You stay here."

She opened the gate, jogged up to the house, pushed open the screen door, and stepped into the kitchen.

"Hey, Leens," her dad called from the living room, as the door whined shut.

"Hey, Dad."

"There's mac and cheese on the stove."

Lena picked up the pot, then opened the fridge, took out a jar of sliced pickles, and spooned some into the mac and cheese, which was the tiny-shells kind she liked best. She carried it into the living room and sat down next to her dad. He was watching some kind of cheap-looking History Channel show with a name like *Atlantis: Evidence of Aliens?*, which was the kind of thing he loved to hate.

"Productive day in the woods?"

"Very."

"Really," he said, throwing an arm over the back of the couch. "Do tell."

What Lena loved about her father was that he meant it. He wasn't asking as a prelude to zoning out, but because he had the ability, rare in an adult, to pay close, granular attention to what kids had to say, without making a show of it. He thought the world was fascinating, and as near as she could tell, this alone separated him from the teachers at her school and the parents of her friends, back when she'd had friends—they were still her friends, she had nothing against them, she just didn't want to do the stuff they wanted to do, and also she knew some of them thought it was weird that she and her dad had stopped showing up to church after her mom stopped being around to make them. Or maybe they thought there was something broken about Lena because her mom had left that they might catch if they hung around.

Luckily for everybody, Lena didn't really care. The drift was mutual, or mutual enough. She had the woods, she had her garden, she had her dad's curiosity, and most of all she had her dad.

Lena couldn't figure out how he knew half the stuff he did. There were hardly any books in the house that weren't about fixing cars, trucks, or boats, which was what her dad did for a living. Sometimes he checked out a horror novel from the library, or read something she brought home. But, like, he knew everything about ants—how? When had he learned that they kept aphids as cattle and that the total weight of all the ants on the planet was equal to the weight of all the humans? And why hadn't he ever revealed this vast, random chamber of knowledge until the day last month when Lena wondered idly at breakfast why red ants bit and black ones didn't?

"I made a friend," she said. "A monster." She nestled down into the couch and took a bite of pasta, cheese sauce, pickles.

"What kind?"

"A golem disguised as a bigfoot."

This wasn't that different from their usual banter.

"I don't think I've ever heard of a golem. But that's kind of a strange disguise. Bigfoots are mostly found in the Pacific Northwest."

Lena put the pot down on the arm of the couch. "He's outside right now. You wanna meet him?"

"Maybe tomorrow. I wanna find out if aliens built Atlantis."

Lena stood up. "I'm serious. I brought him home because he needs to ask you a question."

Her dad studied her for a moment, probably wondering how this conversation had gotten away from him so fast, but all he said was "Okay."

From the way he stood up, Lena realized that the beer in his hand was not the first of the evening, but the third. That was probably a good thing.

She stepped outside, and her dad followed. Lena had expected to have the walk out to the fence to prep him a little more, tell him what a golem was—though she was not sure she had a grasp on that herself—but The Golem had not stayed where she'd put him. He was standing ten feet from the door, peering at the tiny green tomato babies in her garden.

"Dad, this is The Golem," she said. "The Golem, this is my dad."

Lena could tell her dad was gobsmacked, but only because she knew him. And only for an instant.

"Evan," he said, extending his hand. "Nice to meet you."

The Golem looked at it, then at his own.

"Don't wanna crush by mistake," he said, then nodded in Lena's direction. "Your daughter cool."

"Yes, she is," said Evan. "Thank you."

"So, Dad," the witch said excitedly, reminding herself of herself revving up to plead for a sleepover back in third grade or whatever, "The Golem needs to get to Kentucky. And I had an idea."

"Okay," he said, in the wary tone he took whenever she pitched him an idea he suspected he wasn't going to like.

Only he wasn't looking at her. He couldn't tear his eyes away from The Golem.

"I was thinking you could borrow the van from the garage, and we could drive him there. Like a road trip. And before you say you have to work— What if you could make eight thousand dollars?"

"Are you . . . clay?" her father asked The Golem.

"Sometimes clay, sometimes mud."

"Dad!" His head jerked over, and she gave him her cleverest smile. "Eight grand. That's what you said digging the new septic field would cost, right?"

"Yeah," he said slowly.

"If you drive him to Kentucky tomorrow, The Golem will dig it tonight."

Evan's eyebrows rose—a good sign. His head swung back over to The Golem. "You gotta bust through a cement plate," he said. "Then dig twenty feet long by ten feet deep. And you're in the leaching field for the old system, so you're gonna get shit all over you. I was gonna rent a jackhammer and a backhoe. You're telling me you're gonna do all that with your bare hands, in a night?"

"Could. Except The Golem can't work for a goy."

"What's a goy?" asked Lena and her dad together.

"Goy is anybody who not a Jew."

"Can't, or won't?" said Evan.

"Say *can't* because mean *can't*. That just how The Golem designed."

"Well, rats," said Lena. "How come you didn't mention this before?"

"Because The Golem have . . . how you say. Oysveg."

They waited.

"Work-around."

"Do tell," said Evan, and Lena felt a little pang, because that was supposed to be a phrase her dad only used with her.

"Could convert," said The Golem.

"I'm gonna become a Jew so you can dig me a new septic field?" said Evan.

"Want to make clear," said The Golem, "Jews not in business of recruiting. And The Golem personally don't give flying fuck. This just . . . business suggestion."

"I never was much for religion," Evan said. He gave a rueful laugh. "Been kind of a problem around here."

"Me neither," said Lena, and that was about the closest she'd ever come to bad-mouthing her mom. Her dad gave her an even look, a look that was trying not to be grateful.

"Can I unconvert in the morning?" he asked.

"No such thing as unconvert," said The Golem. "But you overthinking this. It just, how you say . . ."

"A caper," said Lena. She loved capers.

"A technicality," said her dad.

"That."

"All right," Evan said. "Why not." He looked at Lena. "Okay with you?"

"Yup," she said, and now *that* was the closest she'd ever come to bad-mouthing her mom.

"There is old joke," said The Golem, "that converting to Judaism is most goyish thing can do. It so goyish that no Jew ever done it."

"Who said that? Seinfeld?"

"Judah Loew ben Bezalel. The Maharal of Prague."

"So . . . what do we do?" asked Evan.

The Golem thought about it.

"You have . . . Fuck, The Golem not know how to say in English. Skin on tip of dick—they cut it off?"

"You're asking if I'm circumcised?"

"Circumcised. Yes."

"No, I'm not."

"Okay, so, The Golem got bad news."

"Hold on," said Lena. "Is there anything like that for girls?"

"You in luck," said The Golem. "Back when rules get made, nobody give a shit about girls."

"Great. I'll convert, then, and you can work for me." She spread her arms. "Ready when you are."

"I've never even met a Jew," said Evan.

All of a sudden, there seemed to be fireflies everywhere. The Golem chased them with his eyes like he'd never seen one before.

"Stand on one leg," he said abruptly. Lena obeyed.

"Man once come to Hillel the Elder," The Golem said,

"and ask him to teach whole Torah in time he could stand on one leg." He paused. "This guy real schmuck. He already ask all the other rabbis, and they tell him go to hell. Shammai even hit him with brick. But Hillel greatest rabbi of them all. And he say *What is hateful to you, don't do to your neighbor. That the Torah. The rest just commentary.* Okay, you can stand regular way now." Lena lowered her leg.

"Wait," said The Golem. "Pick up leg again."

Lena resumed her one-legged stance, pressing the sole of her left sneaker against the side of her right knee.

"Also, Jews have duty to repair world. Called tikkun olam in Hebrew. Very important concept, even if Hillel not mention to one-leg schmuck."

"Tikkun olam," repeated Lena, liking the way the words felt in her mouth.

She waited, but The Golem said nothing more.

"So now I'm Jewish?" she asked.

The Golem shrugged. "Enough for shit hole."

29

Tefillin

Miri picked up her phone. Beneath the shattered glass was a distorted, color-streaked freezeframe of Larry David's face—a fossil record of the moment it had died.

"Where's yours?" she called.

"Dunno." Len jerked, and slapped at his neck. The mosquitoes had realized he was a sitting duck. He pointed down at the grass. "In there someplace, I hope."

Miri found it.

"I'm thinking we call the fire department," she said.

"We are not calling the Clowntown, West Virginia, fire department to come and rescue me like I'm some fucking cat."

"What other—"

"How would I explain how I got in this tree, Miri?"

"You climbed."

"Except I obviously didn't. Then they take our names, run our plates . . . and eventually, when they find a dead cop in the woods, guess who they decide they wanna talk to again?"

It sounded a little paranoid to Miri, but that didn't mean it was wrong.

"I'm open to suggestions," she said. "Want me to look up the top-rated local ladder delivery companies on Yelp?"

"Look in the car. There's gotta be something in there I can use to climb down. A rope or something."

"You think the Admor travels with a rope."

"I don't know, Miri! Fucking check!"

The car key sailed out of the tree and landed at her feet. Miri looked up at him.

"A secret rope that we haven't noticed until now. Even though The Golem ripped out all the seats."

Len didn't respond. Miri looked down at the key, then up at him, then ignored the key and walked over to the SUV and opened the passenger door.

"Still just a bag of Butterfingers in the glove compartment," she reported. "Can you use those to climb down?"

She opened the center console, found Daniel's sunglasses, and put them on. They were prescription. She took them off.

Beneath the shallow top tray was a deeper compartment. It was the last location that might have viably housed a secret rope, and Miri popped it open.

Inside was a familiar matched set of velvet bags, one smaller and one larger.

"Huh," said Miri. She grabbed them and backed out of the car.

"Found something," she called up to Len, wedging the smaller bag under her arm—she would not be insolent enough to let it drop to the ground—as she loosened the drawstring on the larger and removed a leather box adorned with Hebrew writing, attached to a base that was threaded through with a long, coiled leather strap a half inch wide.

"You know what these are?"

"Uh-uh."

"Tefillin. Every morning, every Sassov man wraps one around his forehead and the other around his arm and says the morning prayers. Check it out."

She let the coiled strap unfurl; it reached the ground and kept unrolling.

"Holy shit, it's like twelve feet long!"

"It's got to wrap seven times around his arm."

She opened the other bag, let the other tefillah unspool, and felt herself unspool a little too. These were not just leather and paper—they were faith, they were ritual, they were art. The Hebrew letters on the ktsitse were stamped in gold leaf, the boxes and straps wrought from a single piece of hide, the letters on the scrolls written by a sofer who had purified himself in the mikveh before he undertook the task.

The thousand ancient rules governing the tefillin's creation had been considered, debated, opined on over centuries by scholars whose only wish was to act in perfect harmony with the laws of God. Who believed that everything deserved deliberation, and nothing could be left to chance.

It was not just the observance of a ritual that fulfilled an obligation, Miri reflected as the leather, dyed black on both sides, slapped softly against her shoe. It was the process of codifying and perfecting that ritual. When a man strapped on these boxes, he glorified both. And this was equally true whether the tefillin were opulent and finely made like the Admor's, or merely adequate, like her father's.

"What's in the boxes?" asked Len.

"The verses from the Torah where God says that with a strong hand He brought us out of Egypt, and we should bind these words as a sign on our hands and wear them in between our eyes."

"So every day, they . . . literally strap on those words."

"Yes. It's called laying tefillin. My father used to let me roll his back up and put them away sometimes."

"You think they'll hold me?"

"I'm still trying to work out how I feel about using them as rope. They're sacred."

"Yeah, but we're just gonna use the leather."

"Still."

"Should we call Menachem and ask if it's okay? Maybe you can get his permission to fuck girls, too."

"Don't be an asshole."

"I'm just— I'm a little confused about your attitude. I took one for the team, and instead of helping me, you're fretting about, like, the propriety of using the only thing we have to get me down. It's not like we don't have bigger fish to fry—The Golem is going to get to that rally somehow."

He was right, but Miri didn't want to cave so easily, so she decided to see what would happen if she went on the offensive. It was never her impulse, in these kinds of situations; she'd been trying to learn how to do it.

"You have no respect for anything. No culture at all."

Saying something out loud either made you believe it, or

made you realize you didn't. As she stared up at Len, small and absurd atop his branch, Miri felt the barbs harden into conviction, then melt a little as she second-guessed herself.

Now they were just slush, and she was tired of them and herself.

"How about this," said Len. "You get me out of this tree, we stop The Golem from committing multiple homicides, and then I'll enroll in a yeshiva. Okay?"

"Whatever," said Miri, over it. She wrapped a strap around the palm of her hand, gave a tug, and felt the leather yield a little. "No, I don't think they'll hold you."

"They will if I loop one around the limb and then braid the other to the ends. A braid is six times stronger than the pieces you make it from."

"Where'd you hear that?"

"I'm an art teacher," said Len, nonsensically. "Okay— undo the straps, tie them together, then tie one end around a little piece of concrete or something, and toss it up to me. I'll do the rest."

Miri unthreaded the straps from the boxes with as much ceremony as should could muster, then restored the boxes to their bags and put the bags back in the console, because she knew it would drive Len crazy.

It made her think of childhood, of her brothers, of exercising whatever soft power she could by dawdling when others wanted her to hurry.

It had been satisfying then and it was satisfying now.

Less satisfying were the quarter of an hour it took Miri and Len to connect on a throw and a catch, or the ten minutes he spent tying and braiding the straps.

Miri spent the time eating three miniature Butterfinger

bars, seventy percent of which were now lodged in her molars.

When Len was done, a six-foot tefillin rope hung from his branch. That left about twelve more feet from the bottom of the braid to the ground, but if Len managed to climb down to the bottom, or nearly the bottom, that meant he'd only be dropping about six.

"Okay," he said finally. "Here goes nothing."

He grabbed the tefillin with both hands, locked his legs around the tree limb, and slid around until he was underneath it, like a giant koala. Slowly, he released one leg, testing the straps' ability to handle his weight a little at a time.

He trusted the leather in tiny increments, and Miri held her breath and regretted consuming so much sugar so fast.

Finally, after what seemed like hours, Len was vertical again, the limb above him and the tefillin braid supporting him fully.

"Holy shit," said Len. "It's working." He clamped his knees around the rope and lowered himself a couple of feet, then did it again.

Then the braid snapped and Len let out a yelp and hit the ground elbow-first.

"*Fuuuuuuck!*" he roared, rolling over and cradling his left arm in his right hand.

Miri raced over. "I think I broke my elbow," he said, wincing in pain. "Help me get up."

She knelt, not sure what to do, where to apply this help. She put an arm around his shoulders, and somehow, between her effort and his, Len got to his feet, still clutching the elbow in his palm.

"It doesn't hurt that much if I hold it still," he said, then tested the slightest movement and inhaled sharply. "Maybe it's just fractured."

"Do you think you can drive?"

"Do I have a choice?" He nodded at the strewn innards of the bigfoot suit The Golem had left behind. "Can you make me some kind of sling? Something to hold it in place?"

"Sure," said Miri, hoping that was true. She raced over and rummaged through the detritus. There were some large pieces of foam padding that seemed like they could cradle the arm, if she could find something to tie them up with—

Oh, right. The tefillin. Miri grabbed the braid, and as Len sat in the driver's seat with his eyes closed, breathing through the pain, she went about swaddling his arm in foam, then double-looping the leather around his shoulder and forearm and tying it together. She only jostled the elbow once, eliciting a scream that was sharp but short.

"Okay," she said, stepping back. "Directions to a hospital, then?"

"Yeah." Len stared at the tree. "I should've had you drive the SUV right under me. That would have lessened the distance by a little."

"If I'd smashed it into the tree," said Miri, "that would have lengthened the distance to the hospital by a lot."

Len grunted and put the SUV in drive.

"It's fifty minutes to the nearest hospital," Miri reported.

"Then you better have a really good story to keep my mind off the pain."

30

The Second Time It Happens

"This is not a story I normally tell, because it makes me look incredibly bad."

"I like it already."

"Okay, so I'm eighteen. A baby lesbian. I've been on my own for six months, and I have no idea what I'm doing. I still dress like a Sassov, not because I want to but because I have no other clothes. And I just got my job at the bodega, and my own room, after living in basically a squat this room in the back of a pickle factory in Gowanus that I shared with three other ex-Hasids who I met at this monthly meet-up thing I only went to once. All boys. All drug addicts."

"Jesus."

"Yeah, it was bad. They were also porn addicts. They'd just lie on their gross mattresses with their phones in one hand and— You know what, this isn't even the story. Forget about them."

"I hope someday I can."

He merged onto the highway.

"So I get my very first paycheck, which I immediately spend seventy-five percent of *at* the bodega, buying ramen and bananas and stuff with my employee discount, and I decide I'm going to take the rest and go treat myself. I want to say it was about thirty dollars. Oh, and I bought scissors too, and cut off one of my long skirts, and turned a couple of shirts into weird-looking tank tops, because it was finally summer.

"I took the subway to Manhattan, to West Fourth, got a slice of pizza and a soda—which was still a *wild* experience for me, at this point, like an adventure, to just go to *whatever* place, even if it didn't have a Glatt Kosher sign in the window, and just buy something. Then I walked to Washington Square Park and sat on a bench and looked at people and thought about all the freedom they had and how I was one of them now. Nobody was watching me. Nobody was expecting me. Nobody knew I was there. I didn't have to make it home before the last shift ended and the foreman locked the pickle factory.

"I don't know if you can imagine how that felt, after growing up the way I did, but it was incredible and terrifying at the same time. It was like I didn't know if I was flying, or just falling from really high up."

"Too soon."

"Sorry. So I'm sitting there, and out of nowhere, a salsa band starts to play. I didn't know it was a salsa band then— I didn't know *what* it was. But they've got trumpets, trombones, drums, different kinds of drums . . . and all of a sudden, all the people in the park start dancing. And they all know what they're doing—they all know the steps. All these couples. It didn't occur to me that maybe they'd come there to hear this band—in my mind, they all just, like, happened to be in the park and magically knew how to dance salsa, and this was all totally spontaneous, and it was just one more thing about the world I didn't understand."

Len smiled. "That's adorable."

"And then a girl walks up and asks me to dance. What she said was *Dance with me, mami*. And she held out her hand. Like it was nothing. And she was *cute*. I told her I didn't know how, and she said *I'll teach you*, and the next thing I knew, there we were, in the middle of all the other couples. Dancing.

"I was terrible, but it didn't matter. We were laughing, and I had my hand on her shoulder, and she had her hand on my hip, and I'm looking around, and *nobody gives a shit*. Her name is Ysenia. She's from the Bronx, and she's a senior at NYU, studying urban planning. We danced for a while, and then she was like, *Let's go get a falafel*. And the next thing I know we're walking to the falafel place, holding hands. It was all so effortless. She just . . . picked me up, like it was the most natural thing in the world. Like every day she strolled into the park and chose a girl she liked and left with her." Miri paused. "Have you ever done that? Picked somebody up like that?"

"I don't know," said Len. "Maybe."

Miri waited for more, because it was a weird answer, but all he said was, "Keep telling."

"We stayed out until four in the morning. The city felt

like a playground with her. She was friends with the door guy at the Blue Note, so we just strolled in for free and heard the last song of this famous jazz musician's show."

"Who?" Len wanted to know, which struck Miri as beside the point and utterly predictable.

"Joe Henderson."

"Nice."

"Then she took me to a women's bar, bought me a beer even though I said I didn't drink, and kissed me. That was my first kiss, Len. And it happened in a room full of lesbians."

"Auspicious."

"Finally, we ended up on the street in front of her dorm, and she asked if I wanted to come up to her room."

Miri paused and sighed. "Which I knew she would, so I'd been figuring out how to say no for the last three hours. Because I didn't know what I was doing. I'd never . . ."

She trailed off.

"Done anything," Len finished for her.

"Done anything," Miri repeated. "How's your arm?"

"I'll live. Can I have a Butterfinger?"

"Sure." She took one out of the glove box. "Should I unwrap it?"

"Yeah. And shove it in my stupid mouth, if you don't mind."

"Okay."

He snapped it up without touching her, like a petting zoo goat taking a carrot.

"I told her I had to go, and I gave her my number. We started texting, and two nights later, she invited me over to watch a movie. Which is like . . ."

"I know what it means," said Len. "I'm not *that* old."

"So I went. I was so nervous I threw up outside her building. I had to go buy water and gum at the bodega."

"Can I ask a question? What had you told her about yourself? I mean, like . . . you guys were both super young. Wouldn't it have been normal enough to just say *I'm a virgin,* or *I just decided I like girls,* or something?"

"Yes. Totally. But I didn't know that. I didn't know *anything*. I was trying to be a whole new person, and Ysenia was the coolest girl I'd ever met. All I'd really said was that my family was very religious—and I could tell it didn't make an impact. She was just like, *Yeah, mine too, church every Sunday.*"

"Gotcha."

"So Ysenia signed me in, and we went up to her room and . . . it was bad."

"Like, how bad?"

"When I say I'd never done anything, I mean literally no one had ever touched me before. Including me. So when she tried, I *froze*. Like some animal pretending to be dead."

"Understandable."

"She was sweet about it, which made me feel worse. We took a break and watched TV super awkwardly for a while. I was just sitting there trying to think what I could do, because my body just—it wasn't cooperating. So finally, I decided I'd try to . . . do stuff to her."

Miri felt her face redden.

"It's all right," said Len. "You don't have to go into detail. I was a seventh grade boy once. I know what it's like to be stunningly ignorant of the female body."

"I've never actually told anyone this story."

"Well, I'm honored."

"It was— I made her scream."

"You—"

"In pain. Then I got the hell out of there. Like, fast. Without saying goodbye."

"You fled the scene."

"I fled the scene. And then I did something really crazy."

Len waited for her to go on.

"You've got to understand—I was like, *If I don't fix this, it's going to mess me up forever*. I could feel the whole experience sinking deeper and deeper into me, past the point where I could reach it. Becoming trauma. So the next day, I called Ysenia and told her that I had a twin sister named Rivka, and she'd stolen my phone and made the date and then erased the texts, and *that's* who showed up to her place."

Len laughed harder than any man with a freshly fractured elbow had any business laughing.

"You made up an *evil twin*?"

"I said she was crazy. That this wasn't the first time. And that as far as I knew, she didn't even like women—she just did things like this because she hated me."

"Because Mom liked you best?"

"How'd you know?"

"Just seems like the obvious move. And Ysenia believed you?"

"Yes—because that's how much of a psycho I came off as at her place. Like a totally different person than the one she met in the park. It was almost—"

She broke off.

"What?"

"I guess I almost believed it myself," said Miri, "because I felt so separate from the way I'd acted. So I made another date with her, but for a week away. And I spent the whole time studying up. I read, I watched porn, I even asked one of my co-workers to tell me everything he knew about, you know . . ."

"Pussy?"

"Yeah. But it turned out he considered going down on his wife a sin, so that was a waste of time. And I just— I meditated. I prayed. I masturbated. I did visualization exercises. Everything I could think of so that I'd be ready, physically and emotionally. It's not like I was in love with her. I just— I felt like this was my last chance to be happy or something. It was weird."

"Yeah, that's not the weird part. So? Did it work?"

"Oh yeah. It worked big time."

"You knocked it out the park?"

"I'm— Yeah, sure, I guess. But meanwhile, I had to keep the twin thing going. So I bought a burner phone from my bodega, and I called Ysenia as Rikva, and apologized for pretending to be Miri."

"I can't believe I tried to give you advice about lying to your boss. You're a criminal mastermind."

"Well, not so much. Because instead of saying, like, *What you did was terrible,* Ysenia told Rivka she wanted to see her again. That she had something important to tell her.

"So I went and met her, as Rivka. She took me—took Rivka—to the same bar she took me to the night we met. And she's like, *I know you're not usually into girls, but I've got to tell you, I think you and your sister are both incredibly sexy and it really turns me on to think about fucking twins, so . . .*

*why don't we go back to my place and try again, and it can be
our secret?"*

"Oh my God! That shady motherfucker!"

"Right?"

"So what did you do?"

"I went back to her place and tried again and it was our
secret."

"Did you do it, like . . . the Rivka way?"

"Yup. I was terrible. Maybe worse than before. Which
was . . . this is gonna sound weird, but . . . therapeutic.
Like, what's that expression? The first time something happens it's tragedy, and the second time it happens, it's farce."

"Don't know that one. Damn! So then what?"

"The next day I waited for her outside her building and
confronted her. I was like, *I know you saw my sister*. And she
was like, *Bitch, you don't have a sister*."

"Holy shit. What did you say?"

"Ysenia did all the talking. She was like, *I just wanted to
see how far you were gonna take this shit. You're crazy as fuck.
Bye.*"

They passed an Exit sign. The hospital was only ten
minutes away.

"And that," said Miri, "is how I lost my virginity."

31

Who the Scorpion Is

he Golem sat hunched in the back of a cargo van
bound for Kentucky. He had been thoroughly
hosed off, but he still smelled vaguely of shit.

Len, his fractured elbow properly diagnosed and dressed
and slung, tore down the same freeway. Miri sat beside him,
a bag of snacks and energy drinks between her feet.

The Save Our History's Future rally was scheduled to
begin in another two hours, at eight o'clock sharp, and many
enthusiastic defenders of the Southern way of life had already descended on the municipality of Wagner, much to
the delight of the local eateries and Officer Chadson Nutebridge, who had been placed in charge of crowd control by
his pud-thumper of a commanding officer.

Nutebridge, in turn, had requested all the manpower
the department could muster. He had twelve officers at his

disposal; everybody but Masterson, whose wife had just had a baby and who'd chosen to avail himself of the full twelve weeks of paternity leave because the man was a massive pussy.

Thirteen men to corral a thousand seemed light on the surface, but these rallygoers were good men, family men, Christians. Were they coming to raise holy hell? Yes. But Nutebridge didn't doubt for a moment that they would respect his authority, understand that any order he issued was in service of the common good. Besides, there would be a critical mass of folks he knew and trusted personally—not just his brothers in blue, but six different chapters of the Venerable Order of the Knights of Southern Rectitude, men bound to him by a common cause and a solemn oath.

And best believe, every single one of those boys was coming heavily prepared.

When the cameras rolled, Nutebridge wanted everybody watching at home to see plenty of firepower. To know that the people of Wagner and their friends from near and far carried their guns like they carried their values—proudly and right out in the open.

You wanna take 'em away?

FAFO, as the young buck Carthage was fond of texting.

Nutebridge had had to look that one up, old fogey that he was, but he'd smiled when he learned what it stood for.

Fuck around, find out.

His first order of business this morning had been to haul out all the traffic barricades and build a pen for the so-called media, not overly big or comfortable, modeled on the ones President Trump had at his rallies. It was a genius idea, separating them out like that, so the people could see who their enemies were, and those enemies could know the feeling of being watched for a change. Nutebridge's own innovation was gonna be to pen whatever counterprotesters showed up in with the media. Because why not? You were either a part of this, or you weren't. Whether you came to undermine the rally with a handheld sign or a story full of lies, the message was the same: *You have no power here. You'll stand where we say you can, and if you feel froggy and decide to jump, you'll find out who the scorpion is.*

It was all theoretical, for now. A couple hundred early birds were milling about the plaza, but everybody else was still en route, or hunkered down with posterboard and markers, or putting on their war paint. No cameras yet, and no unfriendlies. Nutebridge leaned against his patrol car, parked on the west side of the plaza for the duration or until the first arrest, and slugged down coffee from his takeout mug.

It wasn't *whether* it was gonna get doctored up with a few belts of Wild Irish Rose from the flask in the glove box, it was *when*.

Just because you were working the Christmas shift didn't mean it wasn't Christmas.

Hell, now was as good a time as any. Nutebridge unlocked the cruiser. Ho ho ho.

The run of show, as presented to the Wagner PD by the Save Our History's Future rally's official organizers, Jeff T. Hudley and Marjane Wampblossom—neither of whom actually existed, because why use a real name and put your real ass on the line when it was just as easy not to—called for a peaceful march around the plaza where the embattled statue of Judge Harrison Grandfield Pettibone stood.

Fourteen times for the fourteen words was the plan, hashed out last night around a raging bonfire at Marshall Grimes's place with key members of the Knights, Identity Evropa, the League of the South, the National Socialist Movement, Patriot Front, and the Fellowship of God's Covenant People—key members plus a few new recruits, who always got a special welcome, an extra serving of hospitality.

The fourteen thing was a touch cutesy for Nutebridge's taste, but symbolism was important to movement building, and inside jokes and codes helped forge identity. For some of these young bucks, today would mark the leap from online to frontline, and the more it felt like the first day of the rest of their lives, like stepping into a brand-new suit of bad-ass armor and joining an army of brothers, the better for the cause.

No sooner did he think it than he heard, "No way! Mr. Nutebridge?"

It was a kid he'd met last night at Grimey's and taken a real shine to. Eric was his name, fresh-faced and all of seventeen, so newly red-pilled that he still wore his hair in a stupid little ponytail at the nape of his neck. He'd traveled here alone, all the way from the top of Indiana—read about Save Our History's Future in *The Daily Stormer* and felt called.

"Hey there, buddy," said Nutebridge, clapping him on the shoulder.

"You didn't say you were a cop!" Eric's blue eyes danced in his head, taking in the badge, the belt.

This was exactly why Nutebridge and the rest of the PD had kept mum about their jobs to the young bucks last night—the surprise reveal was a laser show.

"Look around," said Nutebridge. "You'll see a lot more familiar faces in the blue." He pointed. "There's Blanchard. Carthage over there."

The kid got it, without Nutebridge having to say another word. *We are the government. We are the law. We are America. Welcome to the good fight.*

He could almost see Eric's spine turn to steel.

"I like that T-shirt," Nutebridge told him, pointing at the star-spangled script that read *It's Okay to Be White*. A legend underneath, so small you'd have to be about six inches away to read it, read PAID FOR BY THE 1488 PROJECT.

"Got it on Amazon," Eric said.

Nutebridge gave him a tick of smile. "Try to stay off Amazon, brother. We got places of our own to shop, without helping the Jews get richer." He pointed at a short steel rod strapped to the kid's leg. "Whatcha got there?"

"Tactical baton. Check it out." With a flick of Eric's wrist, it tripled in length, became a thing you could do real damage with. "Cool, right?"

"Very," Nutebridge said. "Now go on, go meet some people. I gotta get back to peacekeepin'."

Eric saluted—weird, but Nutebridge liked where his head was at—and walked off into the crowd. Nutebridge watched him ease right in—hell of a metaphor right there, because coming together was what this was all about—then turned back to surveying the plaza.

The paperwork said the marchers would carry small flames, candles and the like, to symbolize keeping Southern heritage alive. The joke there was that when you came down to it, who was to say how small was small, or how big wasn't? Apply for a candle and bring a torch. The sworn officers of the Wagner Police Department sure as shit didn't intend to hassle you.

After the march, there would be brief remarks. The director of the local historical society was on the docket, and Judge Pettibone's grand-nephew. Neither was actually going to speak, but those names wouldn't raise the hackles of a jerkoff like Sergeant Braxton, and as long as Braxton's hackles stayed down he wouldn't be calling the Staties or the National Guard for reinforcement and dogfucking the whole works.

It had worked like a charm.

There was nothing at all in the paperwork about the other planned entertainment: the burning of one life-sized effigy of Dr. Bernard Schloss, the civics professor who had stirred up all this shit to begin with. Building it had been a VOKSR project, and it'd been fun as fuck—took Nutebridge back to making scarecrows with his granddad to keep birds off the corn.

Instead of a picture of Schloss, they'd copied an old cartoon from a book Highland had: the big hooked nose, the beady, scheming eyes, the nasty-looking rat's-nest beard. It didn't matter whether the professor really looked like that; they'd captured the essence of the Jew, that ancient, rodent-like deviousness, that invisible thumb that was always on the scale.

They'd gotten good and shithoused, and arts and crafts day had culminated in a photo op for the ages: the entire Wagner Chapter of the Venerable Order of the Knights of Southern Rectitude waving their johnsons in the Schloss effigy's face like he was about to get a nice big serving of white pride.

Nutebridge smiled at the memory, took a belt of his enhanced coffee, and looked at his watch. Ninety minutes to showtime, and the plaza was starting to fill up. It was like going deep sea diving, which he'd never done but enjoyed watching television shows about: everywhere Nutebridge looked, beautiful schools and shoals of people moved in harmony, gliding past each other in a synchronized dance.

On the north side of the plaza, thirty-some-odd members of Identity Evropa rounded the courthouse in their white polos and khakis, a genius uniform because it was so regular. They didn't need guns; they'd weaponized the outfit of every dad and golfer and mall jockey in America—and when the Jews and Blacks and libs walked past those dads and golfers and mall jockeys on the filthy, mongrel streets of New York and Seattle, it forced them to wonder whether they were flying quiet flags, waiting for the call, every natural-born white Christian either a soldier in disguise or simmering with potential that was just one internet wormhole, one late night *replacement theory* Google search, away from coming to a boil.

Kept their stress levels up, their rates of hypertension nice and high.

Hell, maybe it was the reason Jews couldn't digest milk.

Moving in the opposite direction, toward City Hall, the two groups sliding through each other in a little symphony of contrast—Nutebridge was getting teary-eyed, the symbolism of it all hitting him right in the heart—was an NSM formation in Battle Dress Uniform, all black from their kepi caps and shades to their spit-shined boots. Some carried red shields painted with the Othala rune; others held rifles.

Mainstreamers and accelerationists; white polos and

black hats. Threading past each other, weaving together to form the tapestry that would liberate them all. Nutebridge craned out further, took in the whole scope of the plaza: the MAGA hats and blood drop cross T-shirts and rippling Dixie flags.

The sun was getting low, and the energy was rising. Three or four TV vans had parked on the street, and camera crews were crowding into the pen.

And here came the Wagner Knights, resplendent in their white-and-crimson Celebration Day robes, with the effigy of Bernard Schloss held high. A wave of laughter rippled through the crowd at the sight of it.

And then, as if to illustrate the exact sense of common purpose that was filling Nutebridge with such emotion, someone lit a torch—and across the plaza, his long-lost brother answered with another, as if to say *Yes, I see your flame flickering in the wilderness, and to it I add my own.*

Another torch blazed, and another, and Vanguard America began a mighty chant: "Blood and soil! Blood and soil!"

All over the plaza now, flames were roaring to life. "Blood and soil! Blood and soil!"

Maybe we're not starting at eight, mused Nutebridge. Maybe we're starting right now.

There was a metaphor in that too.

"Stop white genocide! Stop white genocide!"

One chant blended seamlessly into the next, as if it had all been rehearsed.

How many kids like Eric, sitting in darkness all over the country, would see this and feel the call?

"Jews will not replace us! Jews will not replace us!"

The Knights raised the effigy high, and Bernard Schloss

bobbed up and down to the rhythm of the words, his curly hair bouncing, his hay-stuffed arms stiff at his sides.

Scott Abernathy made an executive decision and lifted his torch to the hem of the effigy's pant leg. The flames leapt quickly to his waist, and the crowd roared and pumped their torches in the air.

So much for walking laps around the judge, thought Nutebridge, grinning. Fuck it. Take it right up to eleven.

32

Except Us

Len parked three blocks from the plaza, on a residential street; it was the first space he could find, and he pulled in behind a mud-spattered pickup with a Confederate flag decal and Tennessee plates. They'd skirted the plaza on the way in, glimpsed the milling bodies and the raised signs, then fallen silent as the reality of where they'd come set in.

They sat in the SUV and watched people stream past, listening through the windows as the rallygoers shouted greetings, exchanged hugs.

It seemed like everybody had a gun. Or a shield decorated with some kind of obscure fascist symbol. Or both. Failing that, a T-shirt emblazoned with a racist code. These people sure did love their racist codes.

"6MWE," Len read aloud. "Six million wasn't enough."

Miri was quiet.

"The 1488 Project. Cute. You know what that means, right?"

A long-haired man in a biker vest and a CAMP AUSCHWITZ sweatshirt walked past, an unlit tiki torch in one hand and a Starbucks Frappuccino in the other, holding hands with a woman—Len hadn't seen too many women—whose tank top read ANTI-RACIST IS A CODE WORD FOR ANTI-WHITE.

"Not everybody's into subtlety," said Len.

He turned to Miri. "All right. We stay on the periphery, don't call attention to ourselves, and keep watch for The Golem. If we see him, we get to him before he wilds out, and we say *Look around, nobody's killing Jews, it's gross and scary but it's just a show, a circle-jerk. They're talking to themselves. There aren't even any Jews here for them to kill—*"

"Except us."

"*Except us. Right. So let's go.* And then we take him, and we go."

Miri gave him a stricken look.

"This is a bad plan."

"Well, it's the only plan we've got. Unless you want to turn around and leave right now."

She didn't answer.

"In which case, we came all this way for nothing."

A trio of dudes in combat gear sauntered past. "Look at that," Len heard one of them remark, "somebody came here all the way from New York."

"Fuck yeah," his friend replied.

"In which case," Len went on, "if he does show up and murder a bunch of people, the blood is on our hands."

It wasn't clear to Len that she was listening, at this point.

"Miri? Hello?"

"I still want him to scare them," she said, staring out the window. "I want—"

"That ship has sailed," Len snapped, then thought the better of it. First things first: Get out of the car and into position. Get Miri's head back in the game.

"Or maybe it hasn't," he amended. "We'll see. Let's just— We don't wanna be late, right?"

He opened his door and stepped into the muggy dusk and hoped Miri would follow.

A few paces away, abandoned in the gutter, lay a shield— black, triangular, with a truck tire painted on it in white, and a pitchfork inside that.

Len picked it up. To his surprise, it was light as air, made of molded plastic—a kid's toy, a cosplay prop. The cheap straps that let you bind it to your forearm had snapped.

"Put that down," said Miri, slamming her door behind her.

"Why, what does it mean?"

"Nothing good."

"A disguise—"

He stopped talking as a trio of young dudes dressed like Trump on a golf course jogged past. Len caught a *Hurry, bro, it's starting* on the wind, and then they vanished around the corner.

"A disguise might come in handy. The strap is broken, but I think I could jerry-rig it to my sling with the tefillin."

"No fucking way," said Miri, yanking the shield out of his hand and frisbeeing it halfway across the street. "Just— no."

She started walking.

Len cast one final look at the shield, and followed.

By the time the plaza came into view, the noise was deafening. A roiling sea of humanity surrounded the statue in the center—two, three times as many people as when they'd driven past—and every few seconds another torch flared on, casting the half dozen nearest faces a flickering red as they opened their throats and roared:

"Jews will not replace us! Jews will not replace us!"

"This again?" said Len, stepping into the shadow of a local TV station's van and crossing his good arm over his bad one. It was an ideal spot: they could see the whole plaza, every vector of approach, but they were outside the fray, close to the media and not far from a couple of cops. "Don't they have any new chants?"

Miri didn't answer, because Miri was having a panic attack—her breath rapid and shallow, her body trembling, the color leached from her face.

Len looked where she was looking, and saw what she saw.

Forty feet away, a dude in a red-and-white robe, surrounded by other dudes in red-and-white robes, was holding a giant Jew-puppet on a stick high in the air, while the rest of them set it on fire with the tiki torches they'd just bought at Walmart.

"Hey, Miri—are you okay? You having trouble breathing?"

Maybe it was the wrong thing to say, because Miri's breathing accelerated instantly. Was this hyperventilation? Was any oxygen getting in there? Len wheeled around, overmatched, looking for help, then remembered where he was and stopped.

Too late. He'd caught the eye of the cop by the edge of the plaza, and in the instant before Len looked away, he saw recognition register in the man's face.

He was trained to clock distress, and he'd clocked it.

Fuck.

Len turned back to Miri just as she doubled over with her hands on her knees and vomited a stream of yellow bile onto the ground.

And then the cop was cutting toward them, clearing himself a path, and every single goddamn person within a ten, twenty, thirty-foot radius was watching, tracking his trajectory, because when a cop moved fast in a place like this it meant something was going down, and the chanting and burning were all well and good but these motherfuckers had come here for some action.

By the time he reached Len and Miri, a dozen dudes were following in his wake, and a dozen more had figured out where he was going and gotten there first.

The flames reached the Jew-puppet's waist, and a new chant rose up. "Burn the Jew! Burn the Jew!"

"Ma'am? Are you all right?"

NUTEBRIDGE, the brass nameplate said. He pressed the button on his shoulder mic and tilted his head toward it, ready to call for backup.

"She's fine," Len said. "She's fine. It was something she ate. Thank you."

Some good ol' boy in a Confederate flag T-shirt cocked an eyebrow at the sound of Len's voice, as if he'd heard a wrong note in his favorite piece of music.

"Where you from, buddy?" he asked.

"Easy now," said Nutebridge, stepping closer, boxing the

guy out. But Len saw the quick twitch of a smile cross his lips.

"Wonderin' the same thing myself," Len heard in his periphery. "The both of them look to me like fuckin' Jews."

"Is that right?" It was the Camp Auschwitz biker, pushing his way to the front of the throng. "Answer the man. You a couple of furnace pellets or what?"

Miri straightened, wiped her mouth with the back of her hand, and looked woozily around. Her eyes paused momentarily on an old man with glasses and a rabbinical white beard, and he spat on the ground and called her a nasty Jew whore.

The chant died down, and some asshole Len couldn't see started shouting into a bullhorn.

"We will confront the Zionist criminals who want to destroy our civilization and erase our history! The West was built by the white race, and the white race alone, and we owe nothing to any other!"

They were surrounded now, and the circle was thickening, growing new layers as the promise of violence crackled through the air. The perimeter separating Len and Miri from the crowd was two feet wide and the only thing keeping it from collapsing was the remainder of this inquiry and the collective decision about what came next.

Len looked for Nutebridge—a potential peacekeeper, a mitigating factor—but he'd been swallowed by the crowd.

Or melted into it, Len thought, remembering that lip-twitch.

"If you *wasn't* a Jew," leered a thick ham sandwich of a man in military fatigues, "you'da said *fuck no and fuck you*—"

And on *fuck you* he pushed Len in the chest—not as

hard as he could have, not hard enough to propel Len through the meniscus of the perimeter, but hard enough that he staggered, off-balance, for a single pace.

And in that tiny envelope of time, somebody threw a bottle.

It smashed on the pavement, in the space that had just opened between Len and Miri, and she screamed and darted away, breaking the meniscus herself.

Somebody groped at her ass, and Miri rushed back to Len's side.

"Ir zolt kakn mit blut un mit ayter," she muttered, dark and low, some kind of curse, and Len wanted to turn and say *What are you, fucking nuts?* but no one had heard and it would hardly have made the situation any worse if they had.

"Think you can protect her, Jewboy?" a gruff voice called.

"Burn the Jew!"

A lit torch flew through the air like a javelin and Len jumped back, out of the way. It landed by his feet, throwing off sparks, and Len grabbed it before somebody else could and held it at arm's length, like it could ward off danger.

"Get the fuck away from us!" he yelled.

Right away, he knew it was a mistake. Taking up a weapon had solidified the chaos, firmed the narrative. Len had fast-forwarded past the taunts, the baiting, the fun-and-games, and landed at the moment of no return, when the only question left is who will throw the first blow, the one that opens the floodgates.

The answer came in the form of a searing pain that shot up Len's right arm and made him drop the torch.

Standing before him was a kid—a fucking kid, no older than Len's students—with a baton in his fist and hatred in his eyes and *It's Okay to Be White* written across his chest.

The crowd became a mob, and the mob surged forward to engulf them.

33

The Protocols of the Golems of Zion

An overpowering stench assaulted The Golem, right through the walls of the van. The scent of shit, he didn't mind—didn't love, but could acclimate himself to and eventually cease to notice. This was something else entirely: it was the smell of Jew-hate, and it worked a potent alchemy on him.

He could feel the vigor flowing into his limbs, from some point of origin he had never been able to locate. The world came into sharper focus; the taut wires of his reflexes restrung themselves, tightening until his reactions became so blindingly instantaneous they seemed almost to rely on precognition.

He banged gently on the wall separating him from the goy and the witch, and smashed a hole between their heads. The stench robbed The Golem of whatever subtlety of movement he usually possessed and replaced it with brute strength, and for some reason he always failed to remember this.

The goy and the witch screamed. Some part of The Golem understood that he had terrified them, but in his current state of agitation he could not be bothered to care.

"Stop car," The Golem said. "Witch, open door."

"You just broke my boss's van," the goy complained.

The rage coursing through The Golem was as difficult to regulate as the strength, and as poorly suited to subtlety. Only through tremendous effort did he restrain himself from knocking the goy's head off his shoulders.

"Unfortunate," he said instead, as the witch did what she was told and the stench rushed in.

The Golem stepped out into an ocean of putrescence and quickly located its source: eight hundred and sixteen Jew-haters—The Golem's mind tallied the number instantly—shouting threats and waving flames in the air.

The only unfamiliar part of the scene was the statue, a few feet taller than The Golem, in the center of the maelstrom. The Golem decided he would crush that first, and see what happened.

Beyond that, probably play it pretty much like Prague.

"Go," he told the witch. "Got killing to do."

Instead, she sprang forward and wrapped her arms around his leg. "Thank you for making me a Jew."

"Whatever," The Golem said, shaking her loose. "Fuck off."

There was an eddy in the swarm of Jew-haters that was troubling him, and all at once he saw what it was—who it was.

They were only moments away from being swarmed.

"Why you come, dickheads?" The Golem muttered to himself, and made a new plan. In the moments since he'd thought of it, crushing the statue had grown into an intensely attractive idea, but there was no time for that now, so he let it go and picked up a small boulder lying in the grass that separated the street from the Jew-hater meeting place. It had a little brass plate affixed to it, with writing on it and a picture of some goy.

He lifted it above his head, then changed his mind and brought it down below his waist and heaved it underhand, in order to achieve the trajectory and accuracy he needed.

It arced through the dark sky, plummeted down atop the statue, and crushed it like an aluminum can.

Cheap piece of shit, The Golem thought.

Where there had been a figure, there was nothing now but a giant rock with ribbons of metal leaking out from underneath, the tarnished outside and bright zinc-alloy inside shredded and twisted like oozing metal guts.

The Golem's opening salvo had done its job: frozen the Jew-haters in their tracks, the next chant dead in their throats. Even their scent was different now, an acrid note of fear at the front of The Golem's nasal palate. The eddy surrounding Len and Miri unspooled the instant the boulder flattened the statue, and all over the plaza the Jew-haters spun in vain, trying to locate the threat.

The threat—his senses thrumming madly as he sprinted toward his friends at a ludicrous freight-train velocity— knew it would take them a few moments. He was a lot to process all at once, especially when he was a massive gray blur and about to kill you.

The feeling that perhaps he had become irrelevant, which had nagged at The Golem ever since the machine gun bullets tore him apart at Babyn Yar, lifted slightly as he ran, to hover just above his shoulders. Was there still a place, in this changed world where his people could be slaughtered by the millions, for The Golem?

Seem like maybe yes, he thought, decelerating before the knot of Jew-haters surrounding Len and Miri and parting that meager sea with ease, letting terror do the bulk of the work and flicking aside the ones too paralyzed by cognitive dissonance to flee. Each one he touched bowled over two or three more, and within seconds The Golem was standing before his stupid friends.

"Want to point out," he said, flicking one final Jew-hater back into the crowd, "if The Golem listen to you and not come, both of you be dead."

"If *you'd* listened to *us*," said Len, breathing heavily, his arm wrapped in some kind of bandage and a gash on his forehead leaking blood, "*none* of us would be here."

"We only came to stop you," said Miri. Her shirt was torn, and there were chunks of puke on her pants.

"You couple of real stubborn dickheads," said The Golem. He could feel the Jew-haters' energy shifting; the initial shock and confusion was wearing off and they were sizing him up, wondering what he was, whose side he was on.

Ironically, The Golem didn't look particularly Jewish.

There were enough guns here to cause him some problems, but only if The Golem stood around arguing like a shlimazel, and only if the Jew-haters had the discipline and brains to mount a coordinated attack. So far, the only thing they were pointing at him were phones.

"Bet you feel pretty stupid," he said, "telling The Golem not to kill."

Just then, a Jew-hater loosed a pathetic little battle cry and ran at them with some kind of bayonet rifle.

There was a dumbest guy in every mob.

This one pulled the trigger just as The Golem wrapped his fist around the end of the barrel. The shell exploded inside and the muzzle shattered, breaking every bone in the Jew-hater's hands and throwing bits of hot shrapnel into his face.

He fell to the ground with a different kind of battle cry, and some other Jew-haters grabbed him and pulled him out of sight.

Time to start killing, The Golem thought.

"Stay close to The Golem," he commanded.

"Wait." Len grabbed his arm. "Don't kill anybody. Just get us the fuck out of here."

The Golem looked down at him, incredulous. Just when you thought a person could no longer surprise you, he turned out to be an even bigger idiot than you could have possibly imagined.

"Are these people not a threat?" The Golem asked.

The press of bodies encircling them was growing thicker, confirming The Golem's suspicion that the Jew-haters didn't know what they were doing. Their guns were useless in close ranks; they'd wind up shooting each other in the back of the head.

Except, of course, for the Jew-haters right up front. As if to illustrate the point, one in a swastika T-shirt lifted a pistol, aimed it at The Golem's chest.

In deference to the fact that he was still discussing the

matter with Len, The Golem lunged forward and crushed the Jew-hater's hand instead of his face.

"Yes," Len conceded, as the Jew-hater writhed in pain. "They are a threat. But—"

"Really? What make you think so?" said The Golem, who was not always great at sarcasm but was learning how to pick his spots, and kicked another Jew-hater in the chest as he began to raise his gun. The man crumpled and the gun went off, blowing a hole straight through his gut.

Doesn't count, The Golem thought. His fault.

"You still can't kill them," Len finished.

"The Golem knows what The Golem smells. The Golem has smelled it before."

"Kill them all," said Miri. "Every single fucking one."

Len's head snapped toward her, incredulity slapped all over his face, and insofar as it was possible for The Golem to smirk, he smirked.

"*What?*" said Len.

"The Talmud says *Rise and kill first those who would kill you*."

"Sure," said Len, in such a way that it was clear to The Golem—who had read the Talmud one hundred and sixty seven times—that he had never so much as opened the book. "But it also says *Treat your neighbor the way you wanna be treated*. Right? That's the Golden Rule. And I don't know about you, Miri, but I don't wanna fucking die."

She gaped at him, speechless.

The Golem understood. It was the argument of a child: simplistic and ignorant, but perfect and pure.

He thought about the witch, as he spun to confront a trio of Jew-haters dimwitted enough to think they could sneak up behind him, and sent all three flying with a single sweep of his indefatigable arm. She was the only Jew he'd ever made, in all his long and violent and sporadic years.

And what had he chosen to tell her, as she stood there wobbling on one leg like a stork?

For all he knew, the witch was watching him right now, face pressed to the window of her van as she wondered what it was she had consented to become, what thing was truest of a Jew.

To survive, The Golem thought. What other answer could there be?

Right?

"They don't have to die for us to live," said Len, as if eavesdropping on The Golem's thoughts. "Please. Just try."

If nothing else, The Golem mused, it would be different. He'd been doing the same shit for five thousand years, and where had it gotten the Jews?

"Can try," he heard himself say, wondering if the witch had bewitched him. Or if he had bewitched himself.

Miri shook her head darkly. "I want blood," she muttered, but it seemed that she was only talking to herself.

"Hold on," The Golem said. "Tight."

He bent, scooped up Len with one arm and Miri with the other, folded them against his chest, put down his head, and charged forward with the deepest, loudest roar he could summon from the depths of his gut.

Or his soul.

But probably just his gut.

A path opened up as if by magic, as the Jew-haters scattered before him.

"Hold the line!" someone shouted, so The Golem pivoted toward the sound of his voice and ran straight over him.

Accident, he thought. His fault.

The Golem busted through the last of their ranks, banked hard onto the street, and accelerated until the wind whistled in his ears. In thirty seconds, he was a few hundred yards from the plaza.

"That way!" shouted Len, slapping at his forearm. "The car is over there!"

The crack of a gun rang out, and the window of a truck shattered, two feet away.

Another crack, and this time the bullet flew into the middle of The Golem's back and lodged there—halfway through the thick, tough matter, clay but not-clay, of which he was currently composed, and inches from Miri's head.

The Golem bent, deposited his friends on the ground, and shielded them with his body as another bullet flew overhead.

"Run," he said. "Get car."

He wheeled around before they could respond, and charged back toward the flash of the gun muzzle.

Muzzles.

Three long-distance rifles. Three black-clad Jew-haters lining up their shots across the hood of a truck.

Another flash, another crack, and The Golem felt a bullet pass clean through his left thigh. The flesh sutured itself shut, and he zagged left as the next bullet whizzed by, and then he was upon them and the notion of restraint or mercy was a laughable thing, a fever dream from a distant past. The Golem had spent less than five minutes with the wraithlike spirit of Lilith more than three thousand years ago, and that conversation seemed realer than the one three minutes earlier that had sent him fleeing the Jew-haters instead of slaughtering them all.

He jumped over the truck and snatched two of the rifles out of the Jew-haters' hands and drove them through their chests. The third marksman dropped his gun and ran; The Golem leapt and tackled him to the ground and dropped an elbow that caved in his skull.

He stood, dripping gore, and turned to the plaza to let the Jew-haters feast their eyes.

There were only about a hundred left, the throng reduced to scattered clusters. The abandoned Jew-puppet smoldered from the beard down, a smile on its face. Four other bodies were strewn about too, lying dead where they'd fallen.

It struck The Golem as a wildly insufficient number.

If he moved slowly enough, fewer would run. Some would gawk and others would piss themselves and others would attack. He would surprise the attackers by ignoring them and chasing down the runners, then double back and cut them down.

Hashem willing, The Golem liked his chances of killing every single one.

And the half dozen people with the big cameras—who smelled okay to him, except one guy—could film it all and Miri would get her stupid wish, a famous Golem to scare the next hundred Jew-haters and the million after that. Or he could smash their cameras, although who knew if that would do anything, since information seemed to just fly through the air now and maybe The Golem had already become, what was the term she'd used, a *mysterious vigilante*.

He stepped onto the plaza, and all the Jew-haters seemed to react at once, sprinting and shooting and pissing. The Golem found himself unexpectedly annoyed by the bullets, the arrogance and the lack of fear they suggested, and also the way they brought the trauma of Babyn Yar rushing back—for it was trauma; he saw that now with a new clarity.

And if he had not been unmade, his aleph erased, that meant that he had been *there*, in that gorge, that grave, insensate, in pieces, for the last eighty years.

That would fuck anybody up, The Golem thought.

He grabbed a couple of flaming torches, reared back, and threw them as hard as he could. Each tore through the abdomen of a Jew-hater with a gun, both of them dressed in uniforms like the one who'd jumped out of that car and pulled his gun on Len.

Sistshik. Pey-tsadik. Cops.

And where there were cops there were usually more cops, and historically speaking, cops had never been a welcome sight for the Jews. Or for The Golem.

There was no prayer for a dead enemy, not in any book he'd ever read, but The Golem felt he should say something.

"Gey in drerd un bak beygl," he intoned, *Go bake bagels in hell,* as the rest of the Jew-haters took off at a dead run, became a Jew-hater stampede.

For once, thought The Golem, the Jew-hater stampede was moving in the right direction.

His eyes flicked from one body to the next, mapping

vectors of pursuit and picking out more cops. It had been stupid to kill those two and spook the herd; now he'd have to sprint ahead and overtake them or they'd reach the grid of streets and split up, and probably a lot of them had cars.

Or he could throw something that would crush a bunch of them at once, and maybe scramble their brains so they ran back toward him. His eyes settled on the TV vans and he squared his shoulders and marched toward them.

"Move," he said, waving an arm at the TV people. "Need to borrow van."

Five of them scattered, but one woman held her ground. "Who are you?" she asked, and shoved a microphone at him.

The Golem thought about it for a moment—a moment he didn't have, because the Jew-haters were escaping.

"Mysterious vigilante," he said. "Get the fuck out way."

"Why are you doing this?" she asked, not getting the fuck out of the way. "This is your chance to tell your side of the story."

"Don't say anything!" shouted Len, screeching up beside her in the Grand Rebbe's SUV. "Come on! Get in!"

"Appreciate it," said The Golem. "But have killing to do."

The wail of a siren drowned out whatever Len said next, and a police car rounded the corner and skidded to a halt in front of him.

Miri leaned forward. "Right now!" she screamed, eyes wide.

The Golem sighed, and resigned himself to the fact that the vast majority of the Jew-haters were going to escape.

"Get on your knees and put your hands on the ground in front of you!" the cop in the passenger seat barked into some contraption that projected his voice from a horn on the roof.

Coward shit, The Golem thought. He could smell them both, through the car.

"Mysterious vigilante?" said the goy with the microphone.

"Dude!" Miri beckoned wildly.

"This is your final warning," the pey-tsadik said into his coward-box. "Get on—"

The Golem grabbed the car by its front bumper and flipped it onto its back.

Another siren, far away, was growing louder.

"It really is a fantastic time to go someplace the fuck else," said Len.

"Fine," The Golem grunted, and climbed into the car.

34

Tikkun Olam

Len knew what he had to do, if not when or how. It was going to come down to seizing the moment, capitalizing on some fleeting opportunity or manufacturing one. The fact that he was driving didn't help—though it did give him a measure of control, and maybe he could find a way to turn it to his advantage.

The fact that he was down to one good arm, not so much.

He had time: that was important to remember. They were fifty miles east of Wagner, and nine hundred away from Brooklyn. If Waleed started working on it right now, maybe he could have a large enough joint waiting for Len by the time he walked in the door.

The night was pitch black and moonless, the highway deserted, and the miles were piling up quickly, if not quickly enough; Len imagined them as a growing buffer between death and safety. He was running on fumes, staring longingly at every exit sign with a stick-figure-lying-in-bed symbol.

Miri, on the other hand, was as hyped as Len had ever seen her, face glowing in the light of her phone as she toggled between Twitter and TikTok and half a dozen news sites.

"*Mysterious vigilante* is trending," she reported. "The footage of him flipping the car has gotten more than six million views."

"Six million wasn't enough," said Len, but nobody got it or nobody reacted.

"Oh, wow, *Golem* is trending now too. Some rabbi woman with a ton of followers is doing a thread. You've been ID'd."

"Fuck it," The Golem said. "Maybe terrifying superhero better for the Jews than unknown hunk of clay. Different time, different Golem."

Len had a thought that nearly made him steer off the road.

"What happens if somebody makes a golem while you're . . . here?" he asked. "Can you be in two places at once?"

The Golem shook his head. "No. When The Golem is . . . tetik?"

"Alive," said Miri.

The Golem waved a finger. "No, no. Not alive. The Golem never say alive."

"Um . . . animate? Active?"

The Golem nodded. "When The Golem active, cannot

make another golem. Don't matter if you King Shit Rabbi and do everything perfect. Will just be clay."

"But," said Len, not sure whether to bring it up, "what about Babyn Yar? I mean, technically . . ."

The Golem made a rumbling sound, deep in his throat. "The Golem been wondering that too. Seem like—"

He broke off, and Len could feel the heat, the energy of his rumination. He glanced in the rearview mirror, saw the glint of The Golem's black eyes, lit up by a passing neon billboard for a roadside porn emporium.

"Like the rules have changed?" Miri finished for him.

"Maybe. That above The Golem pay grade. But what The Golem know for sure is, no matter how many other shmendricks try to make, not gonna work."

"That's a relief," said Len.

They chugged along in silence for a moment.

"'Wagner Chief of Police decries violence at far-right rally that left eleven dead, including three officers, says supernatural being is a hoax,'" read Miri. "Yeah, okay dumbass. Millions of people just saw him flip over a car. Good luck with that."

"Watch," said Len. "They're going to spin this so fast. *The left are the real fascists. The Jews are the real fascists.* It's probably up already. You're just not looking in the right places. Search *Golem* plus *fascist*. Or *Golem* plus *terrorist*."

He gripped the steering wheel harder. "It's all going to get worse," he said, and felt the truth of it sink into his body. The SUV felt suddenly airless, but they were moving too fast to open a window.

The Golem leaned forward, into the dim green light of the dashboard instruments, and said, "Everybody who hate Jews must die."

Len jerked the wheel hard to the right, cut across two lanes of traffic and onto the shoulder of the road.

He slammed his foot against the brake, wrenched his arm free of the sling, and twisted at the waist.

And as the vehicle's momentum sent The Golem lurching forward, Len palmed his forehead and smeared the aleph etched there as hard as he could.

"No!" screamed Miri. "Stop!"

The SUV shuddered to a standstill and The Golem tumbled backward, into the cargo hold he'd hollowed out for himself.

"I had to do it," said Len, the pounding of his heart so heavy he could feel it vibrating his eardrums.

A massive truck tore past, horn blaring.

Len undid his seatbelt and climbed over the center console. He crouched beneath the low ceiling and peered at the massive form of The Golem, slumped on his side against the SUV's back door.

A pair of passing headlights lit him up, and Len gasped. The features of The Golem's face had softened into a state of repose, the craggy brow relaxed and smooth. The black eyeballs had retreated back into the depths of his head, making The Golem appear simultaneously blind and all-seeing, like a statue.

His musculature had rounded, disarticulated. He wasn't dead, because he hadn't been alive, but he was no longer shot through with an ineffable vitality, no longer the repository of his people's history of persecution and survival.

He was merely four hundred pounds of stolen clay, lying in the back of a Hasidic holy man's stolen car, inscribed with the Hebrew word for death.

Len's elbow hurt like a motherfucker. He'd refractured it or something when he'd wiped away that letter.

Then his cheek began to hurt worse, because Miri hit him in the face with a surprisingly potent right jab.

"Why the fuck did you do that?" she demanded.

Len pushed past her and opened the door. The air that hit him was hotter than the air inside. It smelled like paving tar and scorched rubber, as if the highway was breathing right in his face.

But at least outside he could stand up straight.

Miri followed, as he'd known she would.

Len touched his face gingerly, then yawned to realign his jaw. He turned to her, cradling the bad arm in the good.

"He wanted to kill everybody who hates the Jews, Miri. He had to be stopped."

She looked at him with fire in her eyes. "Listen to yourself. *He* had to be stopped? What about *them*? What about the people who *actually want us dead*? Who've been killing us for *thousands of years*?"

Before Len could answer, Miri jabbed a finger at The Golem's body.

"You know why it's *truth* and *death*? Because when you kill a golem—"

"I didn't kill anybody," Len said, trying to convince himself as much as her.

"Because when you kill a golem," Miri repeated, undaunted, "you kill the truth. You go back to lying. To pretending we aren't in danger *all the time*."

The highway was still. A moth flitted through the headlight beams and disappeared into the blackness beyond.

"I can just remake him, you know," said Miri. "I'm *actually* Jewish."

Everything hurt. The moth returned, and thwapped straight into the headlight. Or maybe it was a different moth.

Len tried to gather his thoughts.

"You can either kill The Golem," he said slowly, wanting to lay this out right, "or you can kill the antisemites."

Miri crossed her arms and waited.

"And if we kill everybody who hates us," he continued, "we'll be safe."

"Yes. For once."

Len raised his finger in the air like a rabbi. "But we'll no longer be Jews. We'll be something else."

Miri shook her head. "Bullshit. We've always defended ourselves. Ask The Golem. Oh, wait—you can't."

"Defending ourselves is different than killing every Jew-hater."

"You sound like a fucking idiot."

Len spread his arms to take in everything: the road, the night, the moon. The water, somewhere, that neither one of them could see.

"We're supposed to repair the world, Miri. Tikkun olam."

Miri cocked her head and blinked at him.

"Dickhead," she said lovingly, "has it ever occurred to you that maybe this is *how* we repair the world?"

They stared at each other in silence, out of words and a long way from home.

ACKNOWLEDGMENTS

I owe a great debt, or at least a couple of reasonably priced lunches, to Eddy Portnoy, who provided all the Yiddish translations in the book, usually within minutes of receiving texts like "How do you say 'ripped his guts out through his ass' in Yiddish?" Eddy also took the time to proofread the book for accuracy and help me figure out how to eliminate it.

My cousin Matthew L. Kaplan, his wife Kamy Wicoff, their sons Victor and Henry Kaplan and Max and Jed Kassoy, and my daughters, Vivien, Zanthe, and Asa—nine of my absolute favorite people—were frequently distracting while I wrote this book in the living room and kitchen of our shared summer home.

This is the first novel I've written while Jamie Greenwood and I have been together, and I tend to get pretty intense when I'm writing a novel, so I was a little worried. But it turned out to be a fucking blast. Jamie read the new pages every day, which was a new experience for me, and every day I looked forward to watching her read them, hoping she'd laugh and eager to hear her thoughts.

Daniel Alarcón said yes when I emailed him a hasty four-page outline and asked, "Does this feel like a novel?", then reaffirmed it when I sent him the first few chapters. Then he got super busy and to my knowledge has yet to finish reading the book, even though he has time to text back and forth literally hundreds of times every day.

Chris Gabo and Kevin Coval were among the earliest people I spoke to about this book, and their enthusiasm was the booster fuel I needed to start writing.

Josh Begley, too. He and Alarcón also spent a decent amount of time workshopping my previous idea for a novel, which was a great idea that I could never quite make work and now exists as Len's idea for a novel in the first chapter of this book.

The ideas about epigenetics, in that chapter and elsewhere, are informed by the work of Dr. Courtney Morris and our discussions about it.

DJ Frane and Waleed Zaiter were important interlocutors on the subjects of brain chemistry, evolution, and entheogens.

Josh Michtom provided legal counsel on disbarment, as well as a number of absurd topics related to golem liability that didn't end up in the book.

Safia Elhillo hooked up the Arabic in that one chapter.

I'd like to apologize to all the movie execs to whom I pitched the dolphin/LSD/handjob story over drinks by the pool at the Avalon Hotel in Beverly Hills, on a day a few years back when I had like six back-to-back "general" meetings and decided to see what would happen.

Dave Barry and Alan Zweibel were giant impediments to the writing of this novel—and every novel, no matter who is writing it.

The Sassovs' ten-year relocation plan and the machinations necessary to pull it off are ideas Danny Hoch and I developed for a TV project. My understandings of Williamsburg and short-term rental scams also owe substantially to Danny. I'm also grateful to Danny for performing the audiobook.

Dan Charnas, Joe Schloss, and Shawn Setaro read the finished draft, and when they liked it, I was like, *word, maybe I'm onto something here.*

Jason Santiago lent me his beautiful upstate New York home, and I wrote the last few chapters of the book there. To my knowledge he has not yet put up a plaque to commemorate this fact.

My parents, when I pitched them this book over dinner, did not seem to believe I was actually going to write it. As always, though, they are deeply supportive of my work, and I'd like to thank them for that and for a delicious meal.

I talk the most about Judaism to J.PERIOD, Adam Lazarus, and Jamie (again) and I'm very grateful for those conversations. Discussing golems, Jewish literature, and more with Professor Kitty Millet was also generative.

Eugene Cho designed the fly Golem State Warriors logo that we used on all the promo items.

I sent Defcee the book and asked him if he might consider making some music inspired by it. He responded by creating an entire concept album entitled *Telfillin: Inspired by The Golem of Brooklyn*. It's incredible, and I'm so grateful. I'd also like to thank Messiah Musik, who produced the entire project and absolutely laced it, and Alex Fruchter and Closed Sessions for putting the album out.

Thanks to the Jewish Futures Project for giving me some money, and Coava Coffee for being my coffee sponsor.

I'm thrilled to work with Chris Jackson, the sharpest editor on the planet, and I'd also like to thank Avideh Bashirrad, Carla Bruce, Nicole Counts, Lulu Martinez, Andrea Pura, Maya Smith, Greg Mollica, Susan Turner, Ted Allen, Raaga Rajagopala, Elizabeth Mendez-Berry, Sun Robinson-Smith, and everyone else at One World, as well as Richard Abate at 3Arts.

And for the sustaining gift of their friendship—which I realize sounds like I am a public radio station holding a fundraiser—I'd like to thank Bryant Terry, Torrance Rogers, Weyland Southon, Phraze Vader, Davey D, Quency Phillips, K-Dub, Dug Infinite, Bakari Kitwana, Attia Alam, Sarah Suzuki, Josh Healey, Michael Schiller, Antonella Vitale, Idris Goodwin, W. Kamau Bell, Kathryn Borel, David Katznelson, Theo Gangi, Andre C. Willis, Tricia Rose, Johnny Temple, Blake Lethem, and Martín Perna.

ABOUT THE AUTHOR

ADAM MANSBACH is the author of the #1 *New York Times* bestseller *Go the Fuck to Sleep*, as well as the novels *Rage Is Back*, *The End of the Jews* (winner of the California Book Award), and *Angry Black White Boy*, and the memoir in verse *I Had a Brother Once*. With Dave Barry and Alan Zweibel, he co-authored *For This We Left Egypt?* and the bestselling *A Field Guide to the Jewish People*. Mansbach's debut screenplay, for the Netflix Original *Barry*, was nominated for an Independent Spirit Award and an NAACP Image Award and he is a two-time recipient of the Reed Award and the American Association of Political Consultants' Gold Pollie Award for his 2012 Obama/Biden campaign video "Wake the Fuck Up" and his 2020 Biden/Harris campaign ad "Same Old," both starring Samuel L. Jackson. Mansbach's work has appeared in *The New Yorker*, *The New York Times Book Review*, *Esquire*, *The Believer*, and *The Guardian*, and on National Public Radio's *All Things Considered*, *The Moth Storytelling Hour*, and *This American Life*.

adammansbach.com

ABOUT THE TYPE

This book was set in Fairfield, the first typeface from the hand of the distinguished American artist and engraver Rudolph Ruzicka (l883–1978). Ruzicka was born in Bohemia (in the present-day Czech Republic) and came to America in 1894. He set up his own shop, devoted to wood engraving and printing, in New York in 1913 after a varied career working as a wood engraver, in photo-engraving and banknote printing plants, and as an art director and freelance artist. He designed and illustrated many books, and was the creator of a considerable list of individual prints—wood engravings, line engravings on copper, and aquatints.